JOHNNY BOO GOES LIKE THIS

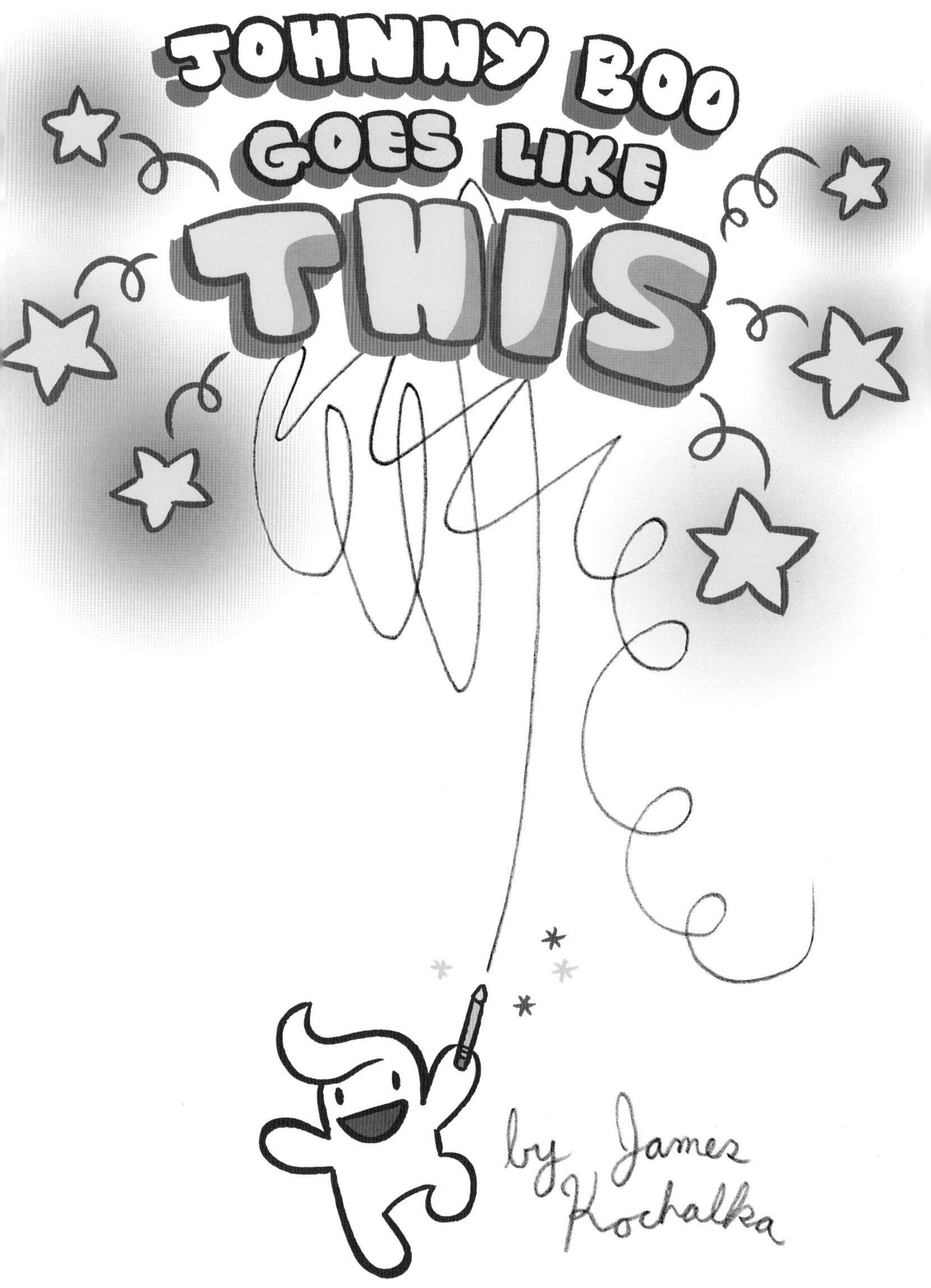

by James Kochalka

TOP SHELF PRODUCTIONS

FOR ELI & OLIVER

KOCHALKA

Johnny Boo Goes Like This! © 2016 James Kochalka.

Published by Top Shelf Productions, PO Box 1282, Marietta, GA 30061-1282, USA. Top Shelf Productions is an imprint of IDW Publishing, a division of Idea and Design Works, LLC. Offices: 2765 Truxtun Road, San Diego, CA 92106. Top Shelf Productions®, the Top Shelf logo, Idea and Design Works®, and the IDW logo are registered trademarks of Idea and Design Works, LLC. All Rights Reserved. With the exception of small excerpts of artwork used for review purposes, none of the contents of this publication may be reprinted without the permission of IDW Publishing. IDW Publishing does not read or accept unsolicited submissions of ideas, stories, or artwork.

Editor-in-Chief: Chris Staros.

Visit our online catalog at www.topshelfcomix.com.

Printed in Korea.

ISBN 978-1-60309-384-2

18   17   16   15   5   4   3   2   1

CHAPTER ONE

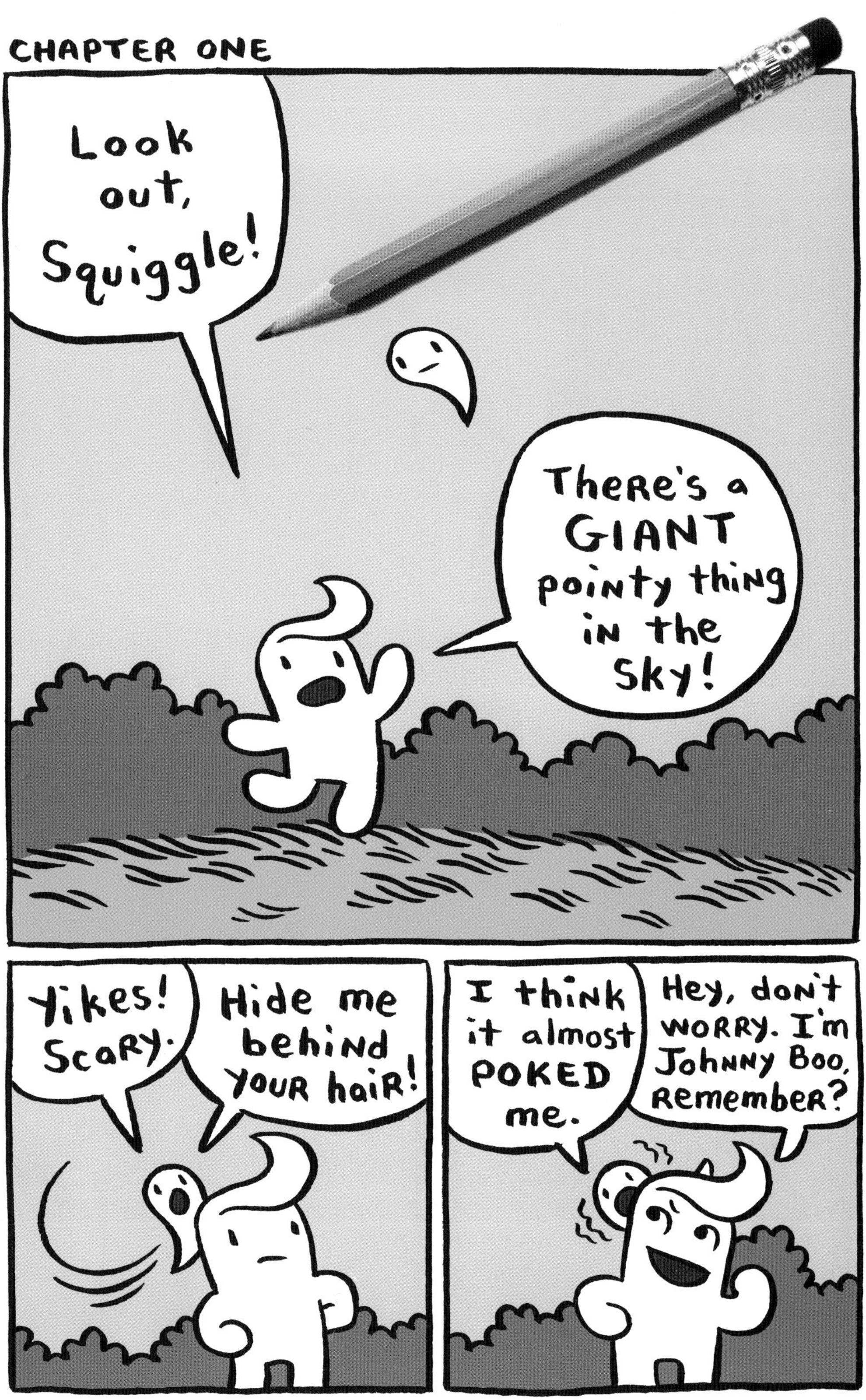
Look out, Squiggle!
There's a GIANT pointy thing in the sky!
Yikes! Scary.
Hide me behind your hair!
I think it almost POKED me.
Hey, don't worry. I'm Johnny Boo, remember?

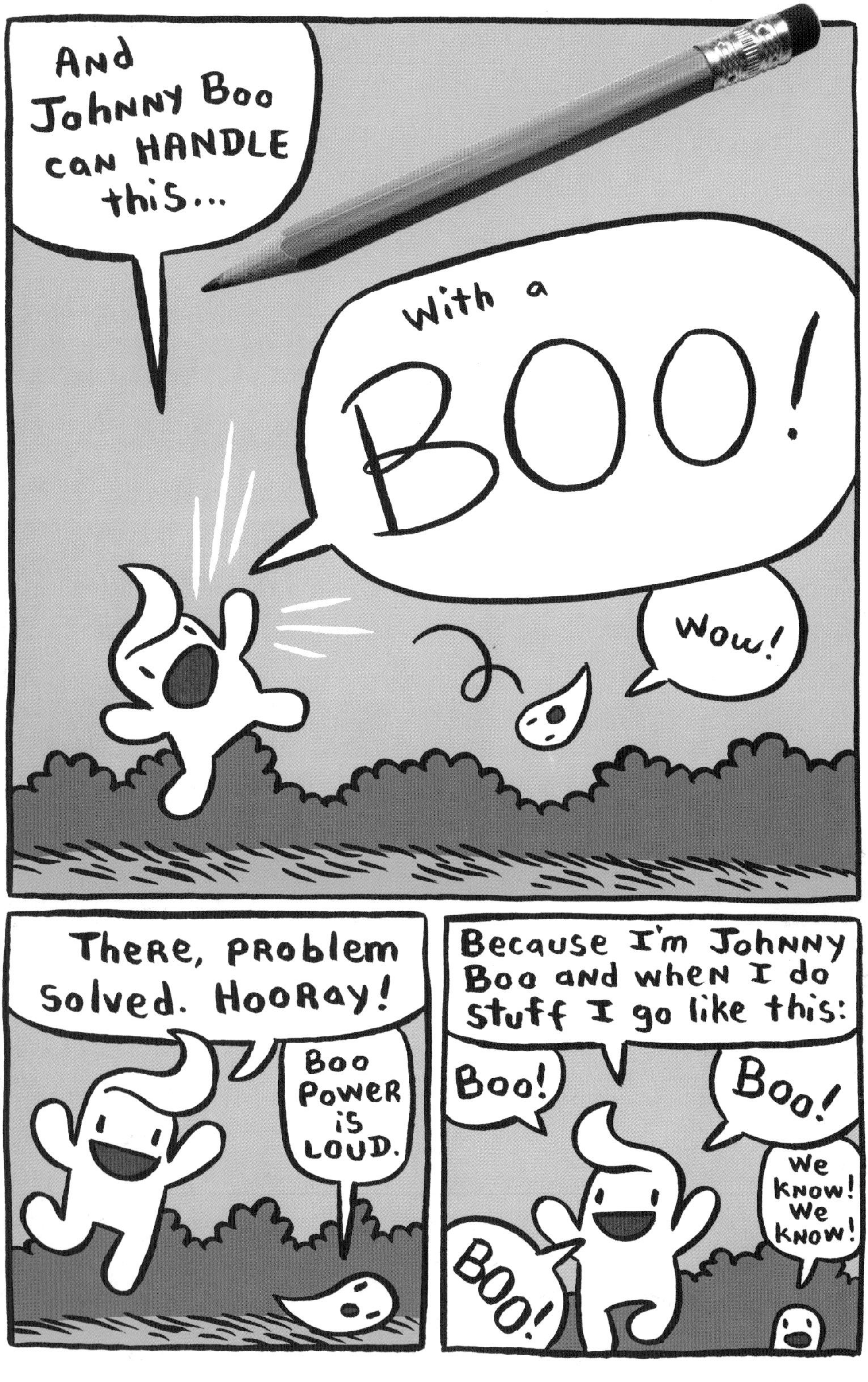
And Johnny Boo can HANDLE this...
With a BOO!
Wow!
There, problem solved. HOORAY!
Boo Power is LOUD.
Because I'm Johnny Boo and when I do stuff I go like this:
Boo!
Boo!
BOO!
We know! We know!

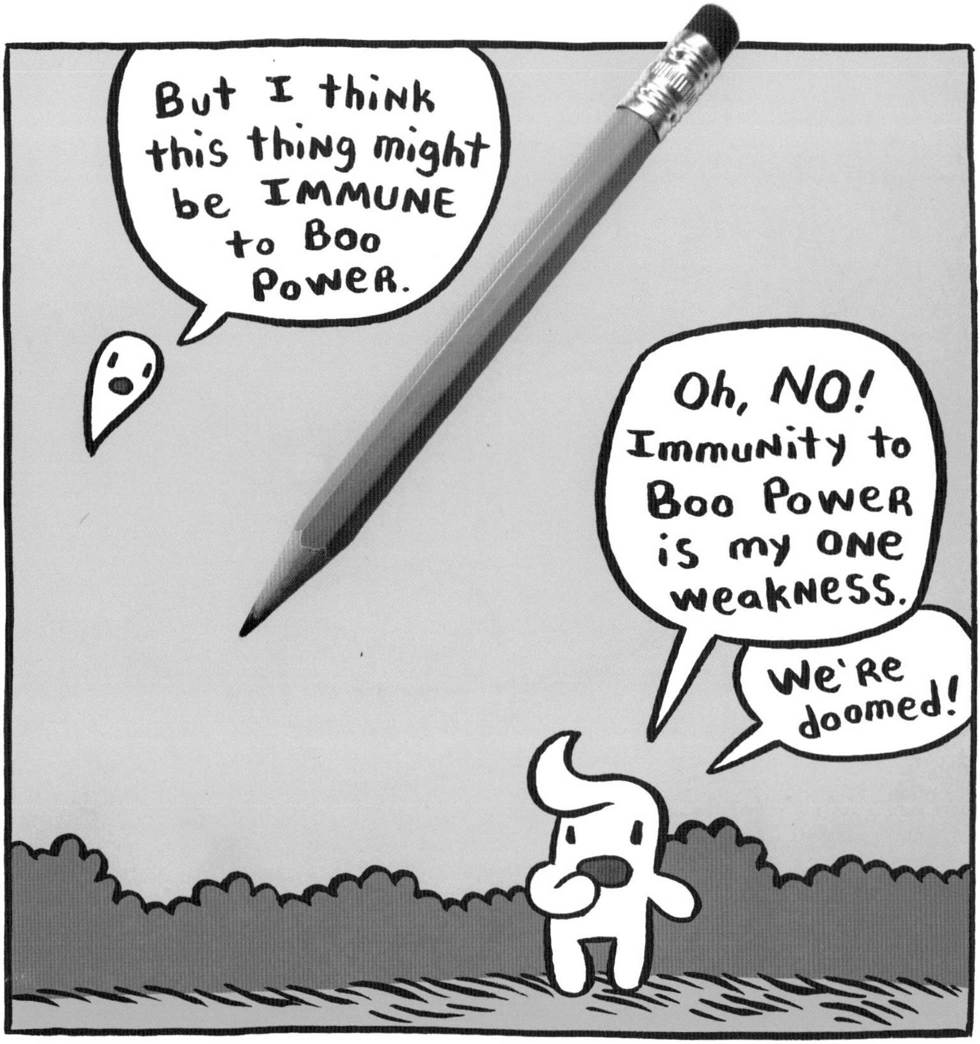
But I think this thing might be IMMUNE to Boo Power.
Oh, NO! Immunity to Boo Power is my ONE weakness.
We're doomed!

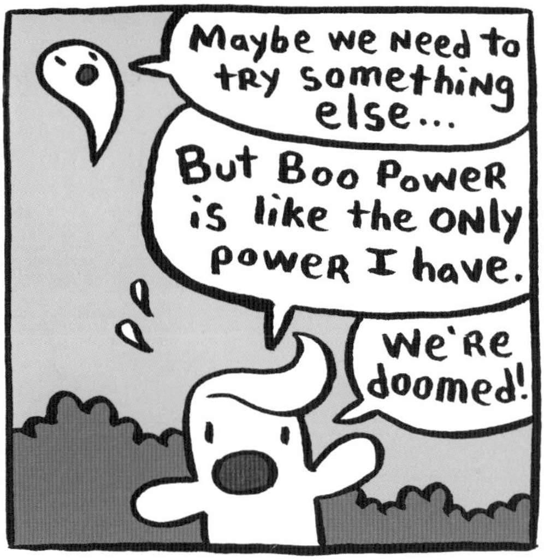
Maybe we need to try something else...
But Boo Power is like the ONLY power I have.
We're doomed!

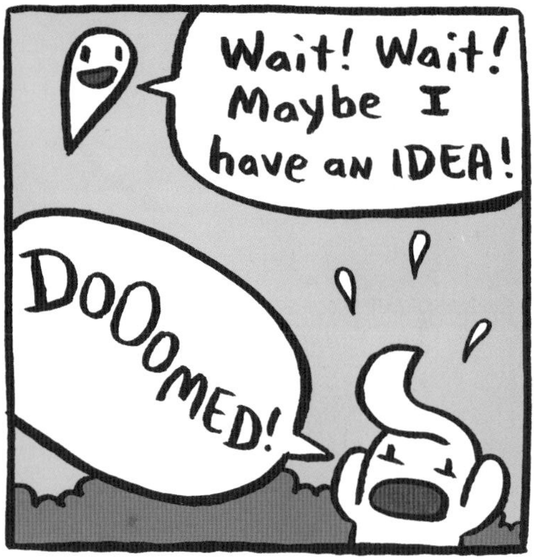
Wait! Wait! Maybe I have an IDEA!
DOOOOMED!

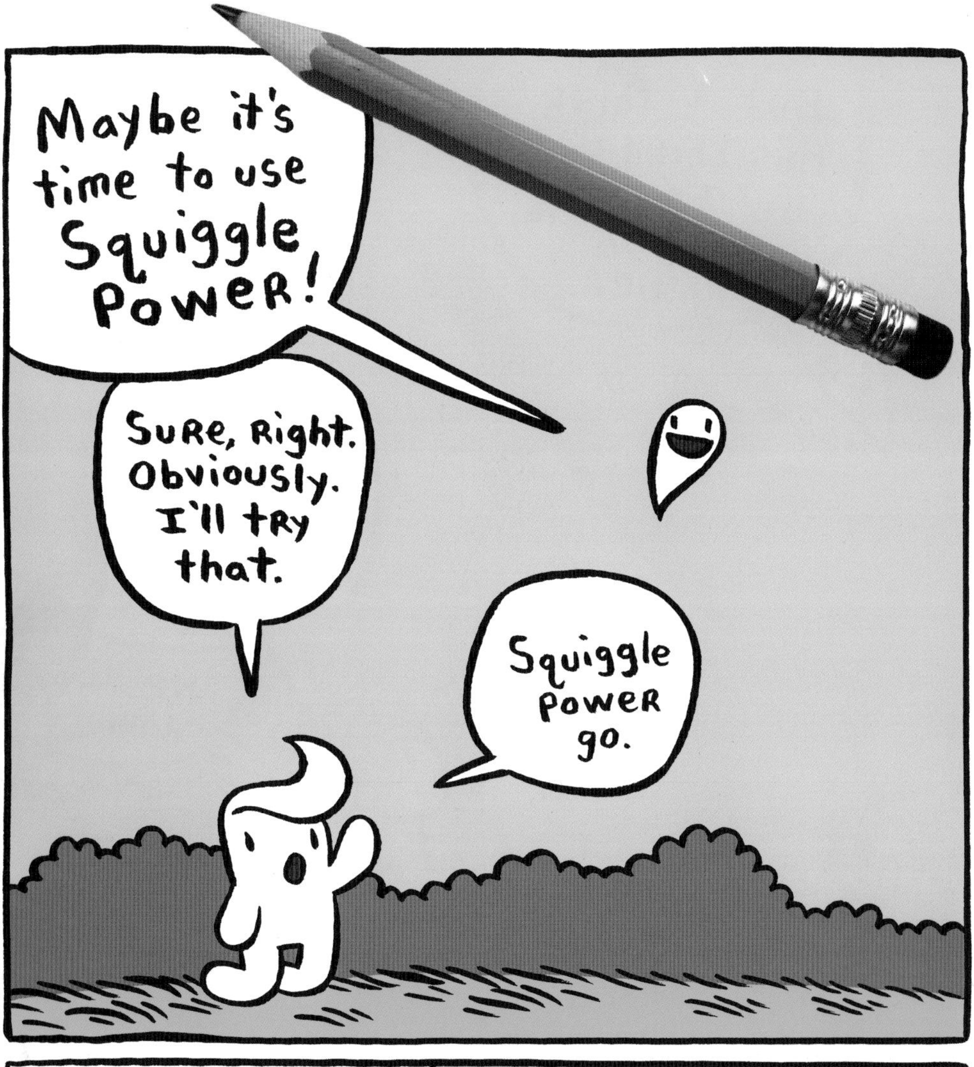
Maybe it's time to use Squiggle Power!
Sure, Right. Obviously. I'll try that.
Squiggle power go.

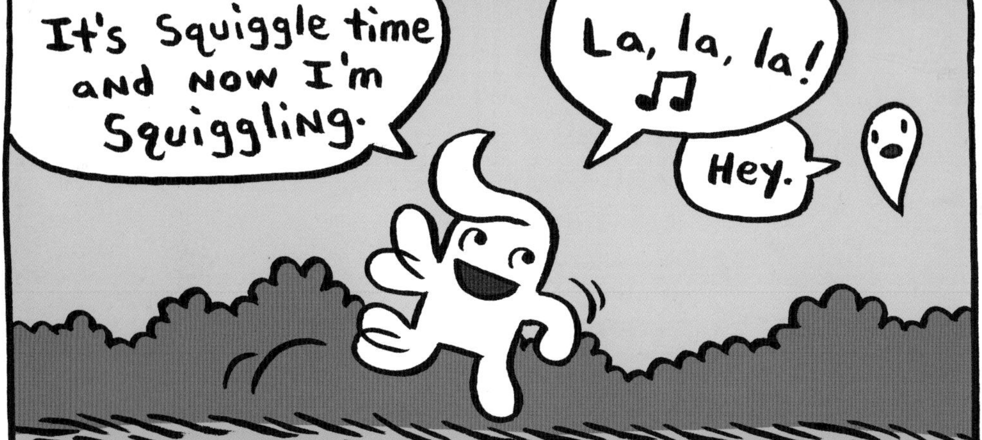
It's Squiggle time and now I'm Squiggling.
La, la, la!
Hey.

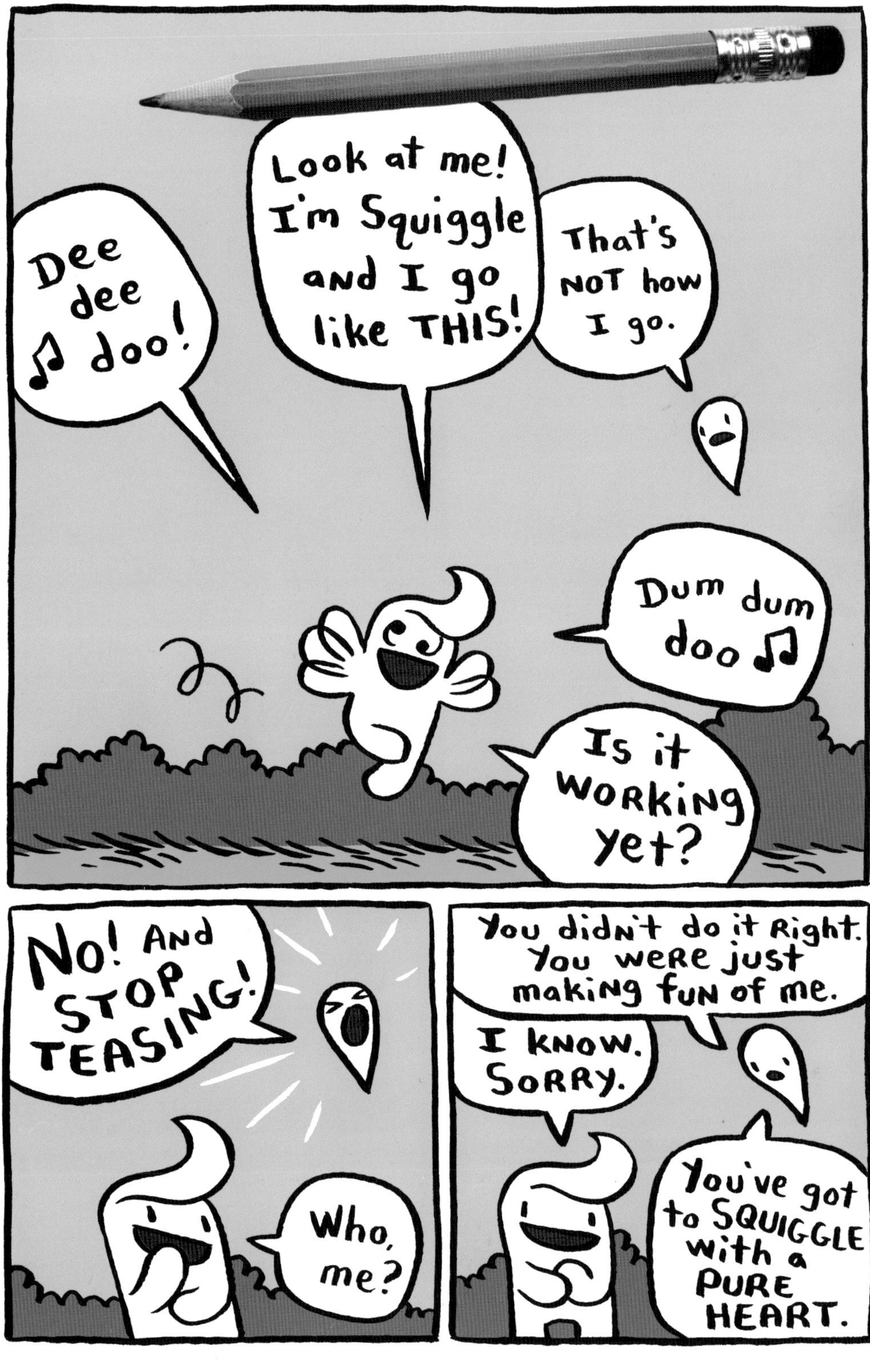
Dee dee ♪ doo!
Look at me! I'm Squiggle and I go like THIS!
That's NOT how I go.
Dum dum doo ♫
Is it WORKING yet?
No! AND STOP TEASING!
Who, me?
You didn't do it Right. You were just making fun of me.
I KNOW. SORRY.
You've got to SQUIGGLE with a PURE HEART.

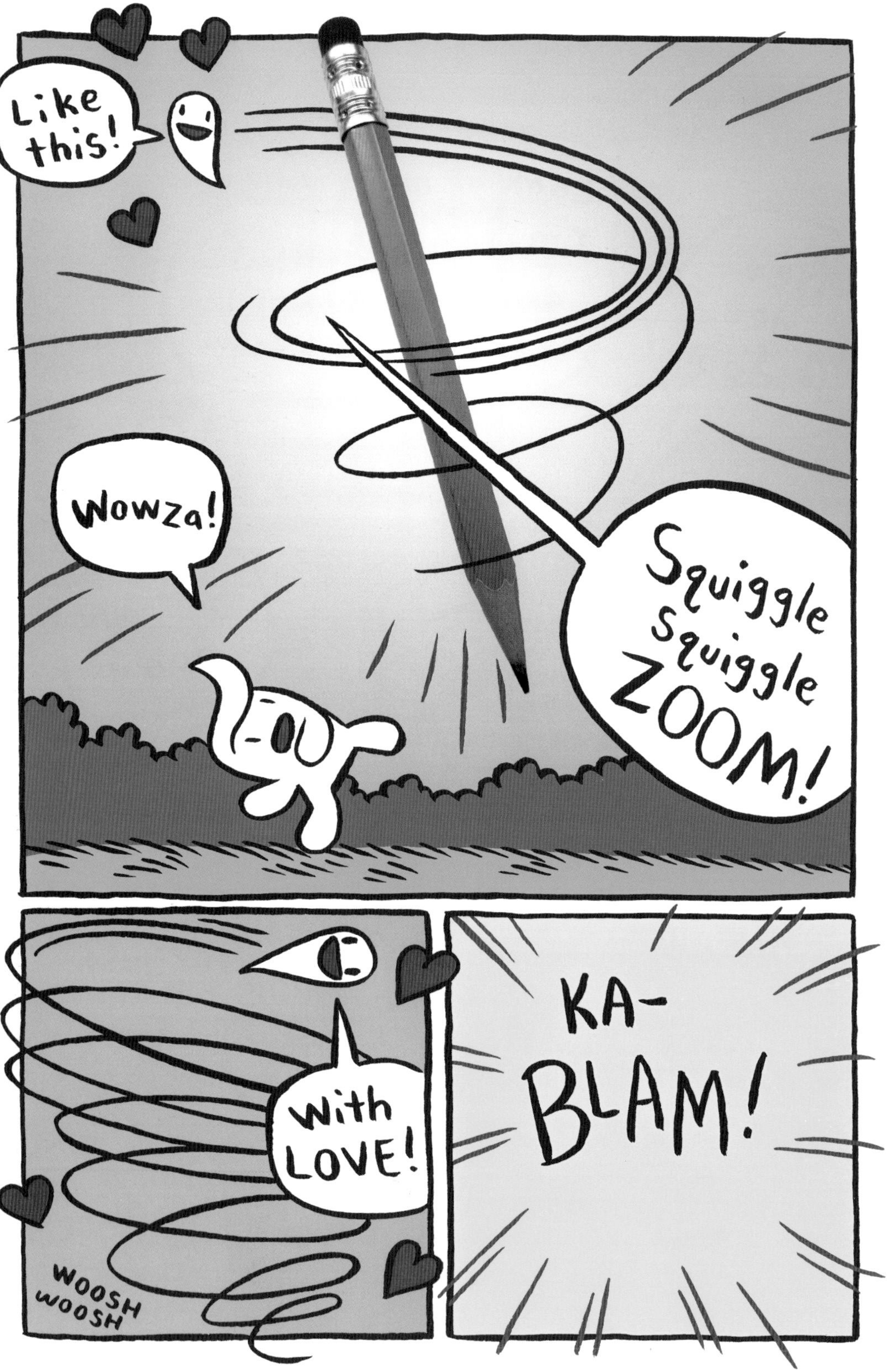
Like this!
Wowza!
Squiggle Squiggle ZOOM!
With LOVE!
WOOSH WOOSH
KA-BLAM!

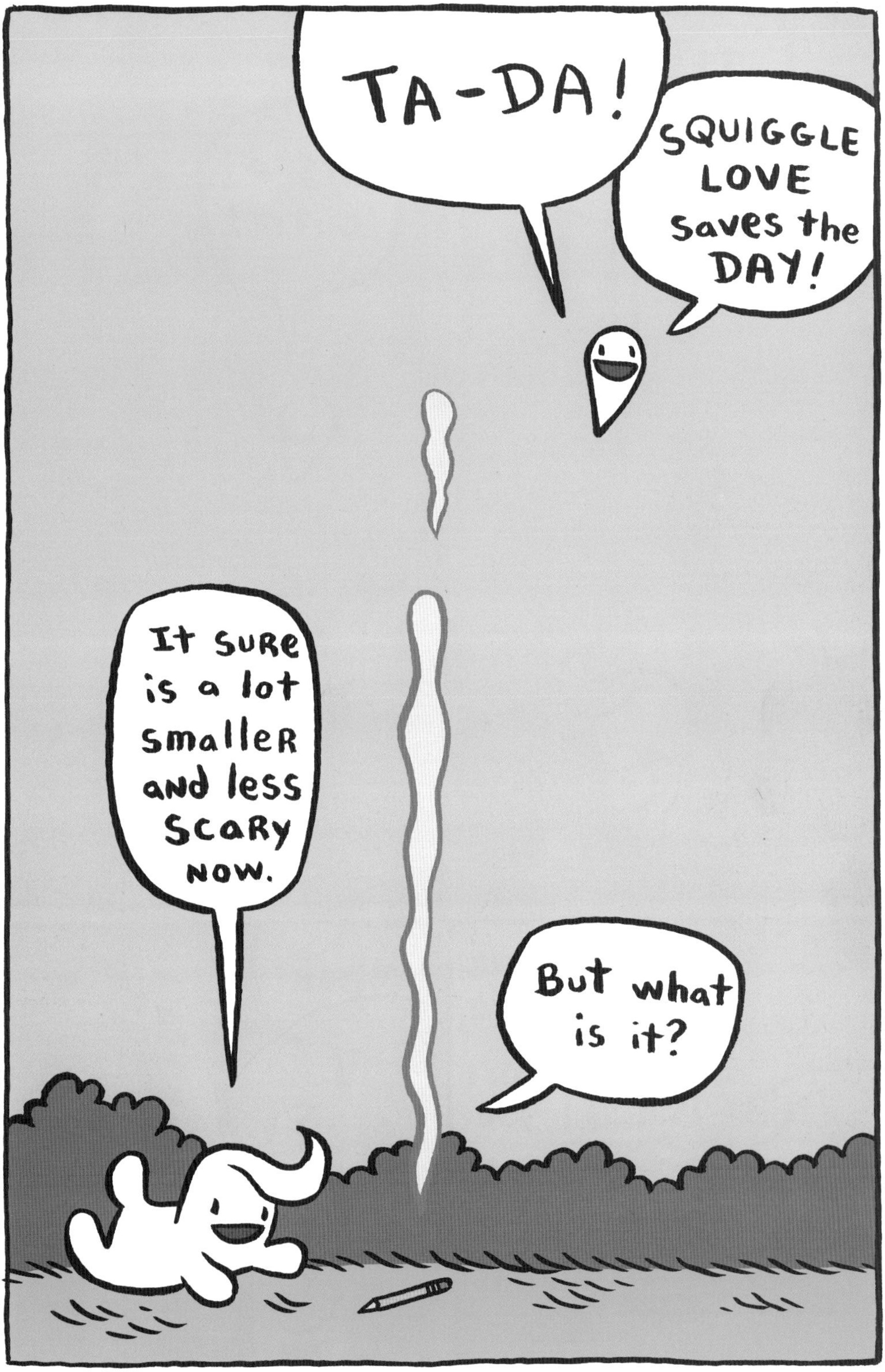
TA-DA!
SQUIGGLE LOVE saves the DAY!
It sure is a lot smaller and less scary now.
But what is it?

CHAPTER TWO

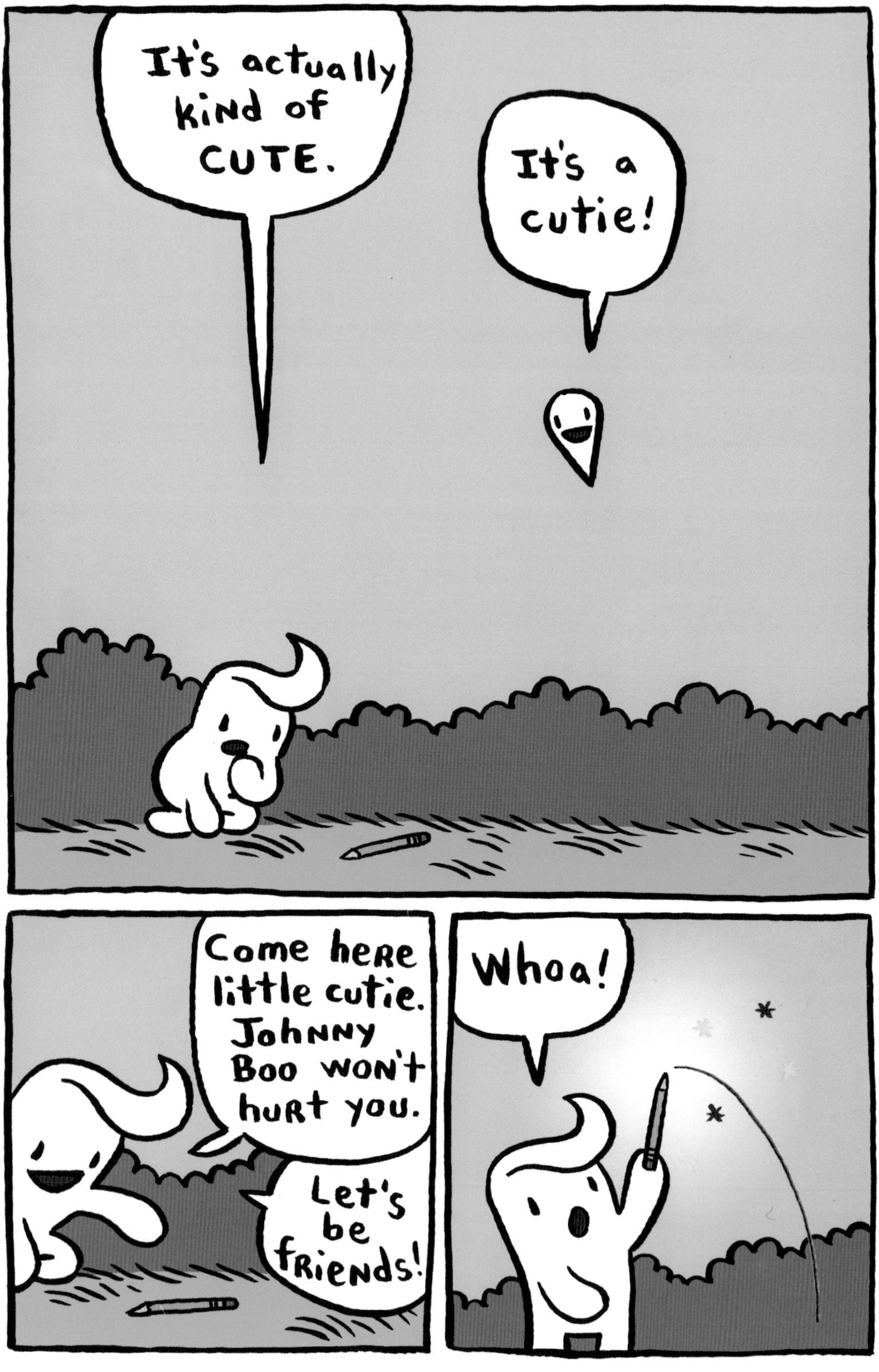
It's actually kind of CUTE.
It's a cutie!
Come here little cutie. Johnny Boo won't hurt you.
Let's be friends!
Whoa!

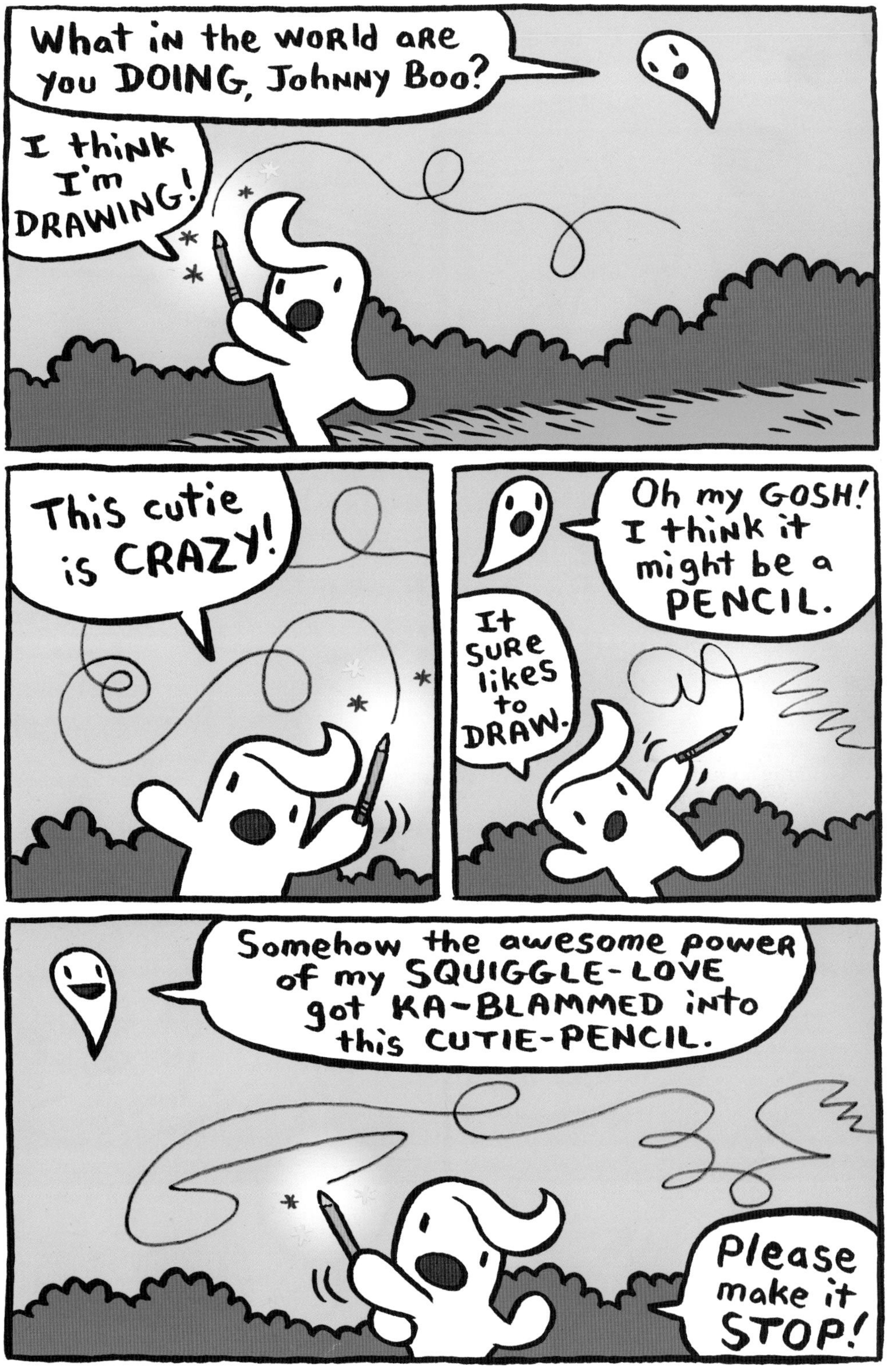
What in the world are you DOING, Johnny Boo?
I think I'm DRAWING!
This cutie is CRAZY!
Oh my GOSH! I think it might be a PENCIL.
It sure likes to DRAW.
Somehow the awesome power of my SQUIGGLE-LOVE got KA-BLAMMED into this CUTIE-PENCIL.
Please make it STOP!

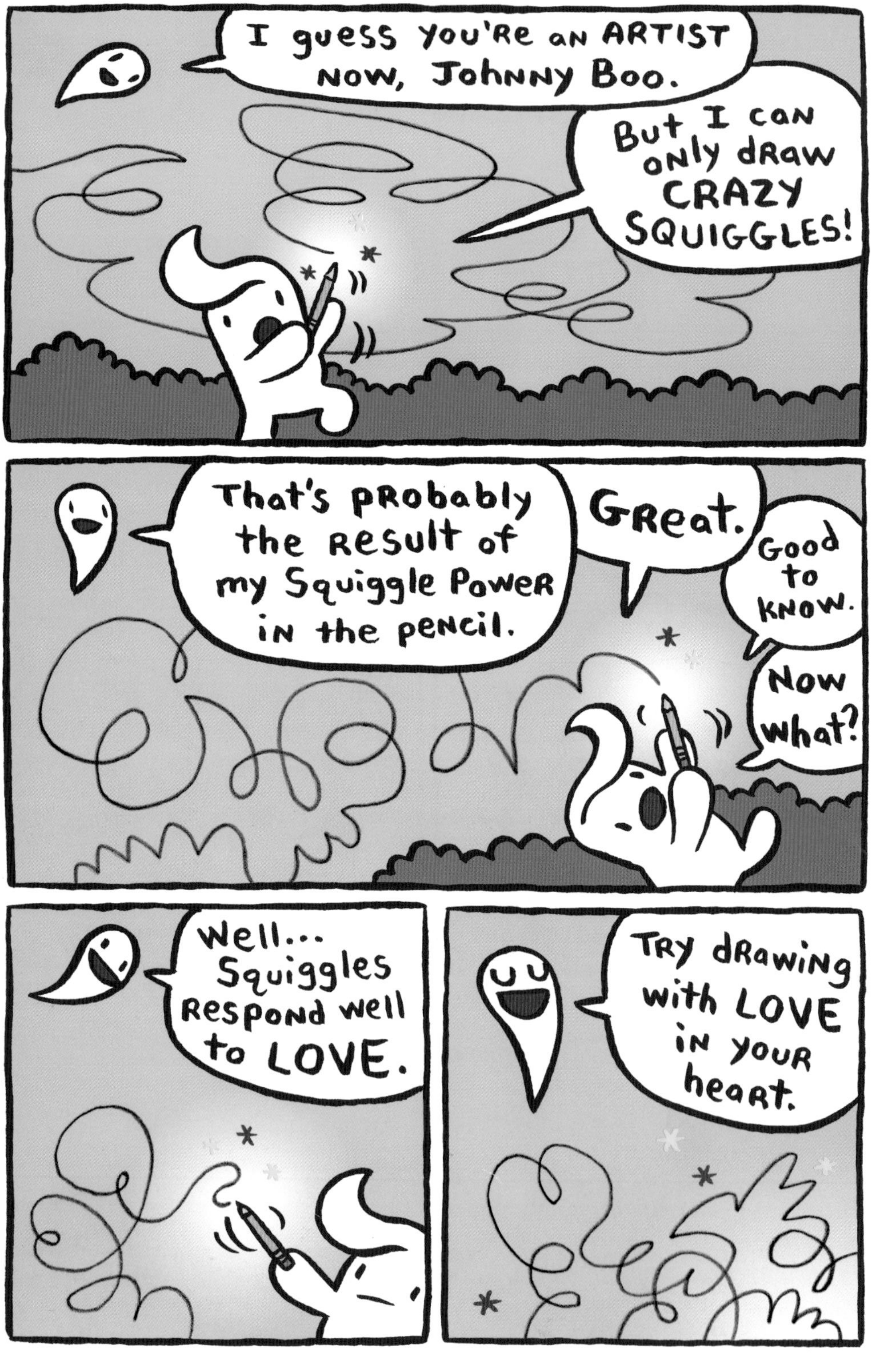
I guess you're an ARTIST now, Johnny Boo.
But I can only draw CRAZY SQUIGGLES!
That's probably the result of my Squiggle Power in the pencil.
Great.
Good to know.
Now what?
Well... Squiggles respond well to LOVE.
Try drawing with LOVE in your heart.

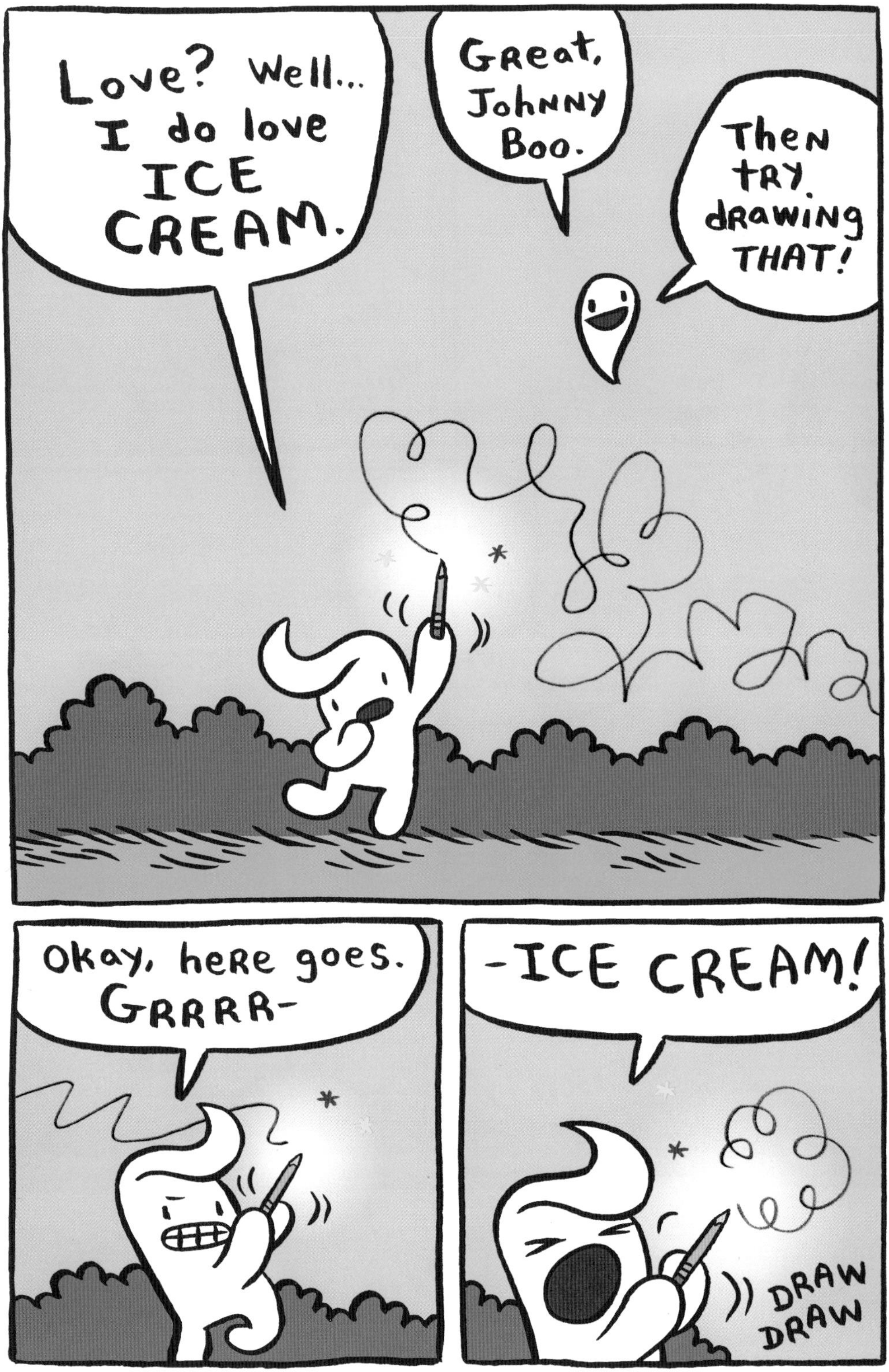
Love? Well...
I do love
ICE
CREAM.
Great,
Johnny
Boo.
Then
try
drawing
THAT!
Okay, here goes.
GRRRR-
-ICE CREAM!
DRAW
DRAW

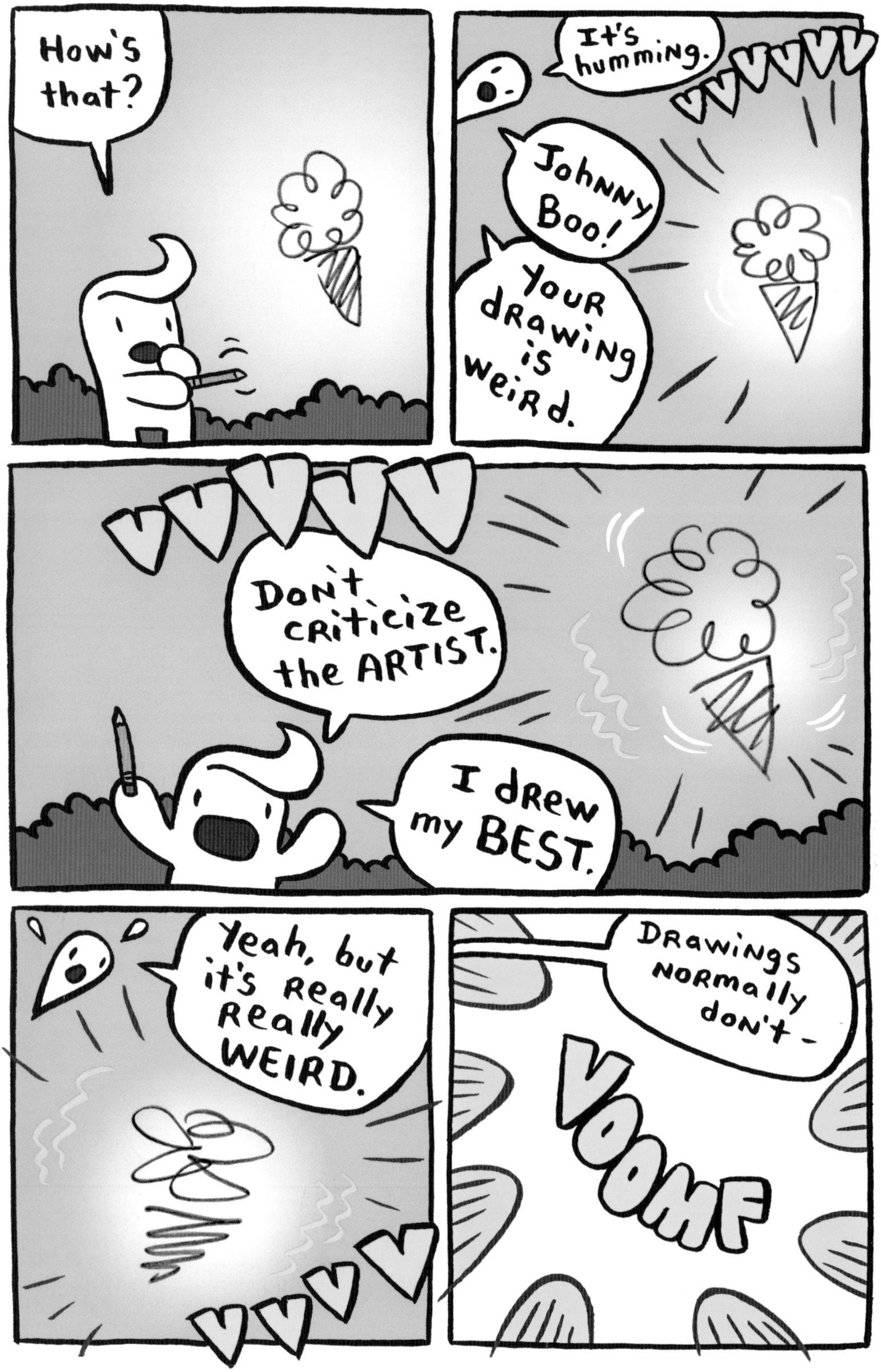
How's that?
It's humming.
VVVVVV
Johnny Boo!
Your drawing is weird.
VVVVV
Don't criticize the ARTIST.
I drew my BEST.
Yeah, but it's really really WEIRD.
VVVV
Drawings normally don't-
VOOMF

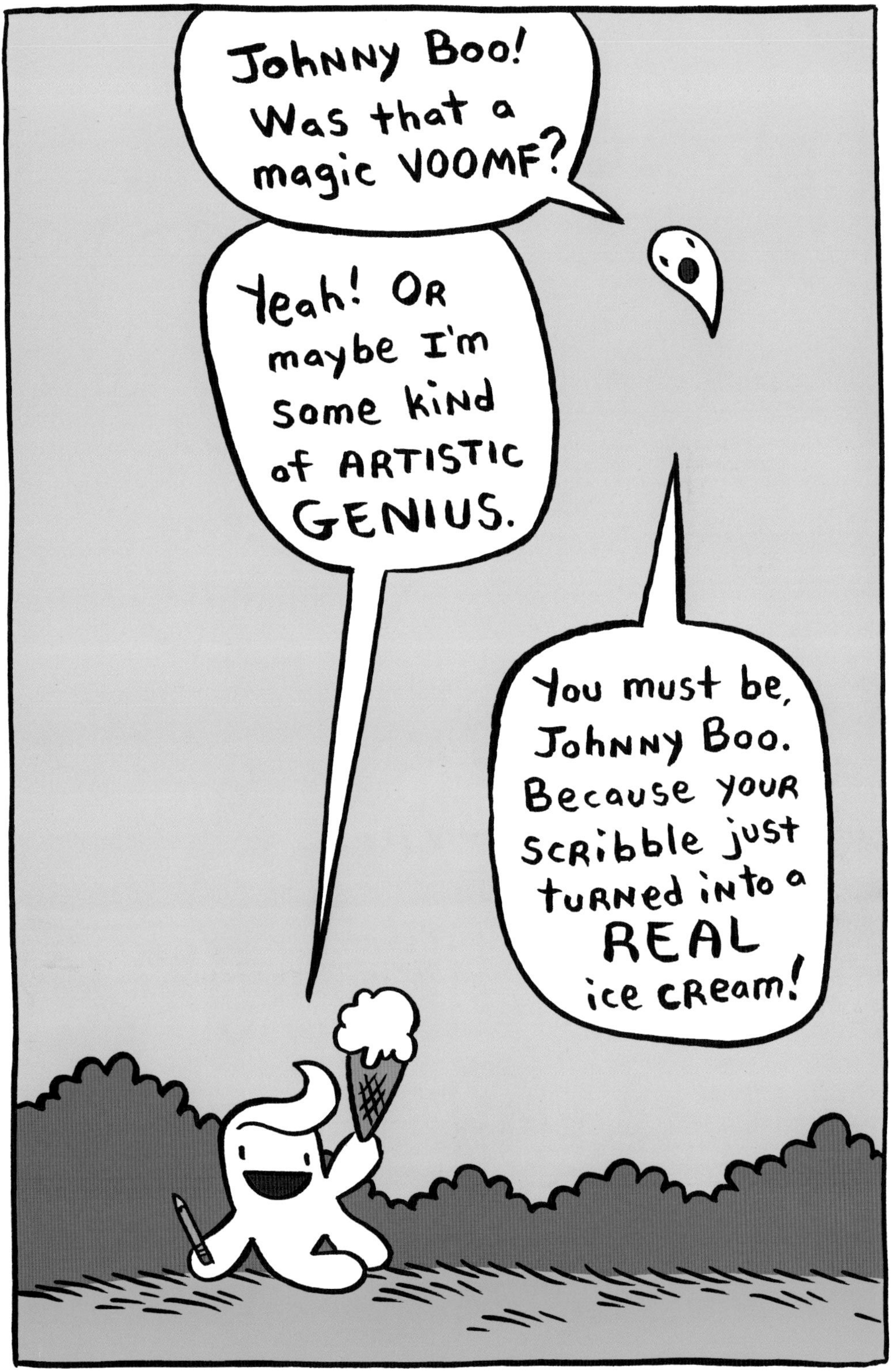
Johnny Boo! Was that a magic VOOMF?
Yeah! OR maybe I'm some kind of ARTISTIC GENIUS.
You must be, Johnny Boo. Because your scribble just turned into a REAL ice cream!

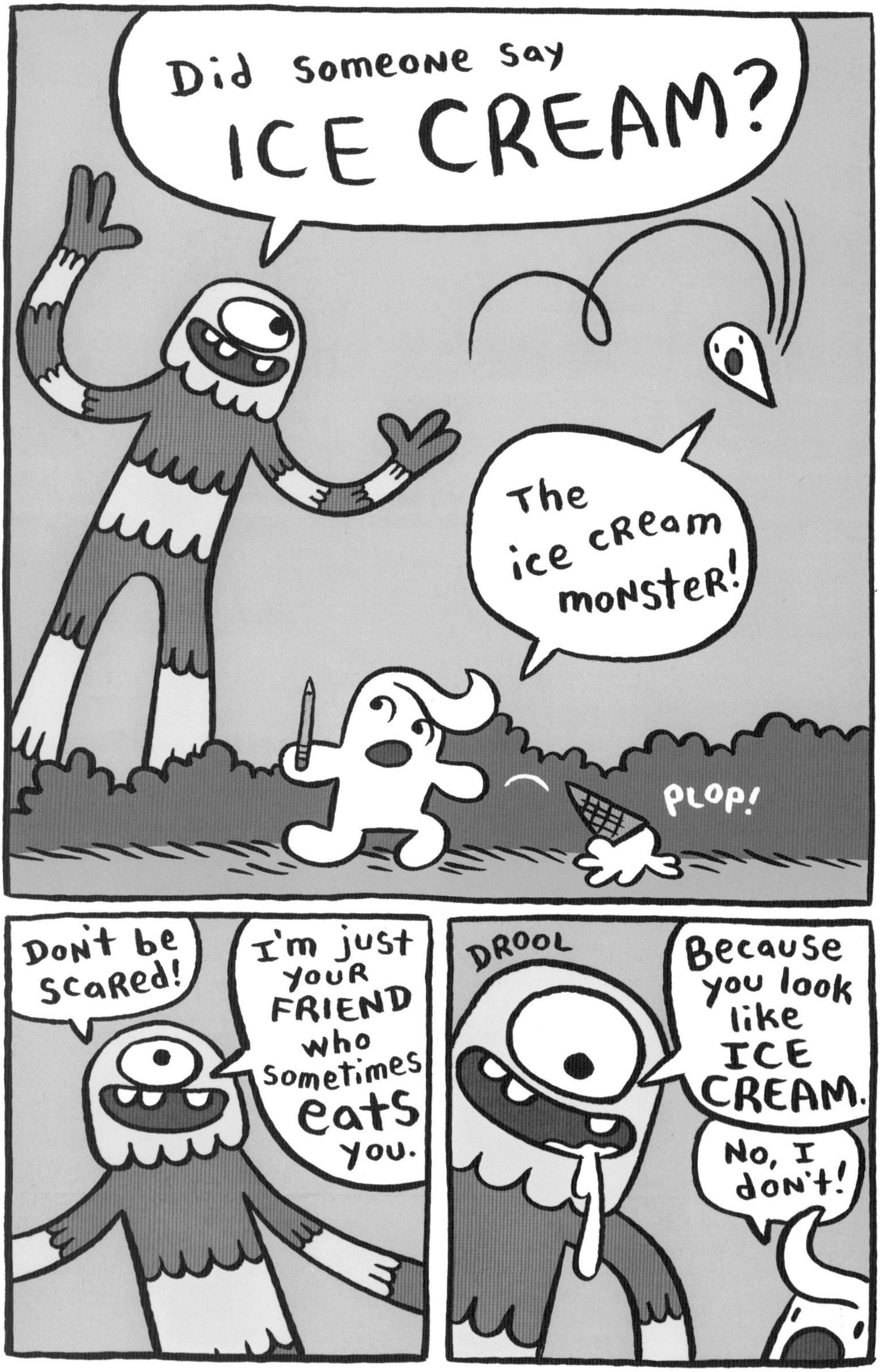
Did someone say ICE CREAM?
The ice cream monster!
PLOP!
Don't be scared!
I'm just your FRIEND who sometimes eats you.
DROOL
Because you look like ICE CREAM.
No, I don't!

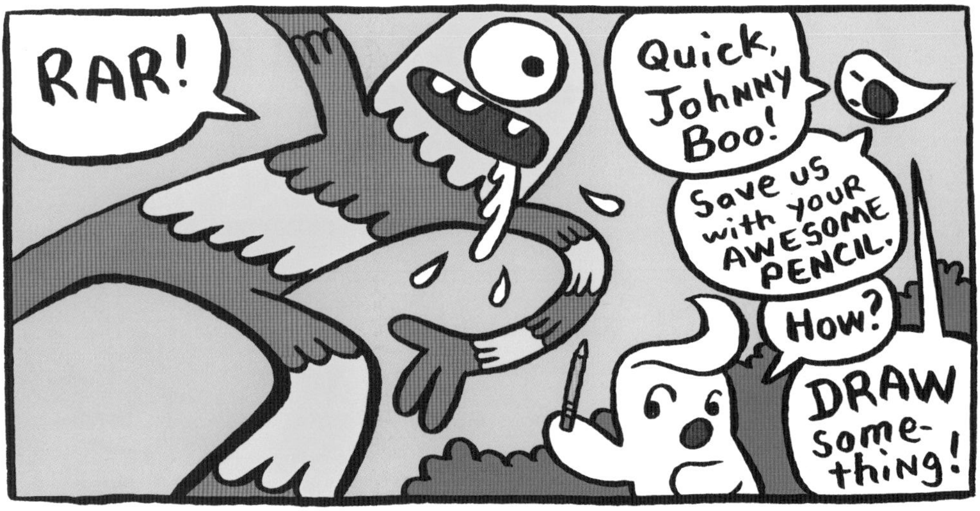
RAR!
Quick, Johnny Boo!
Save us with your AWESOME PENCIL.
How?
DRAW some-thing!

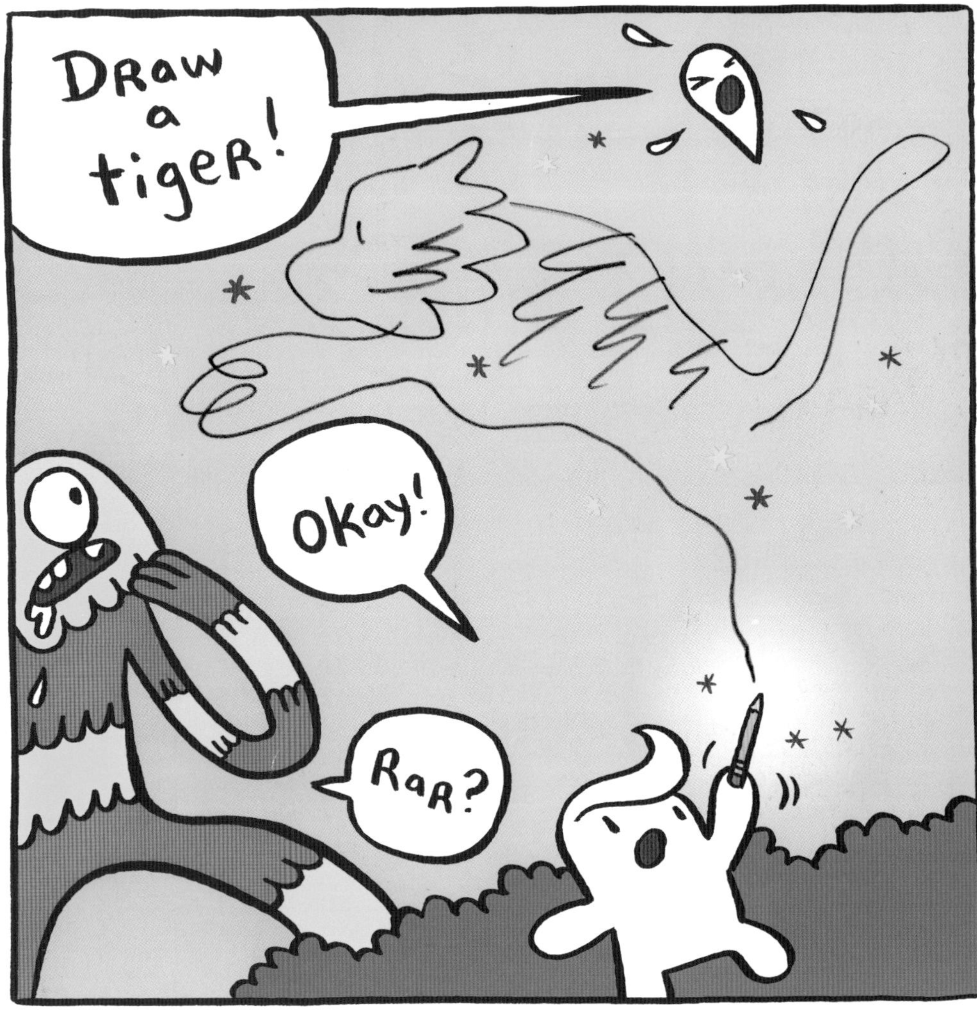
Draw a tiger!
Okay!
Rar?

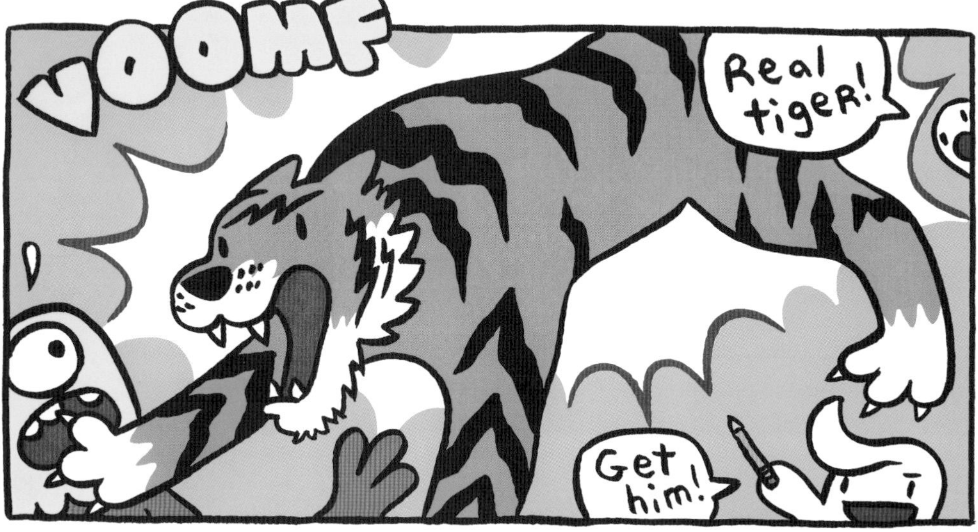
VOOMF
Real tiger!
Get him!

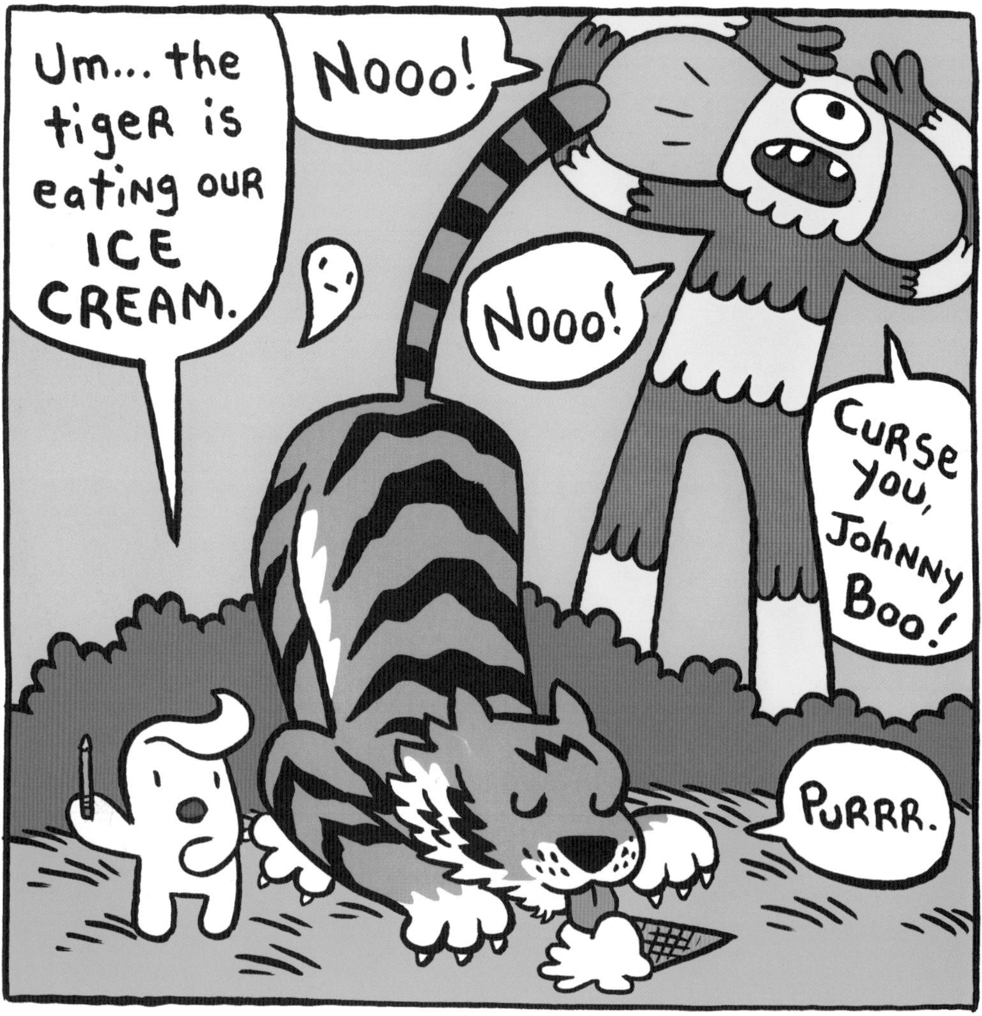
Um... the tiger is eating our ICE CREAM.
Nooo!
Nooo!
Curse you, Johnny Boo!
Purrr.

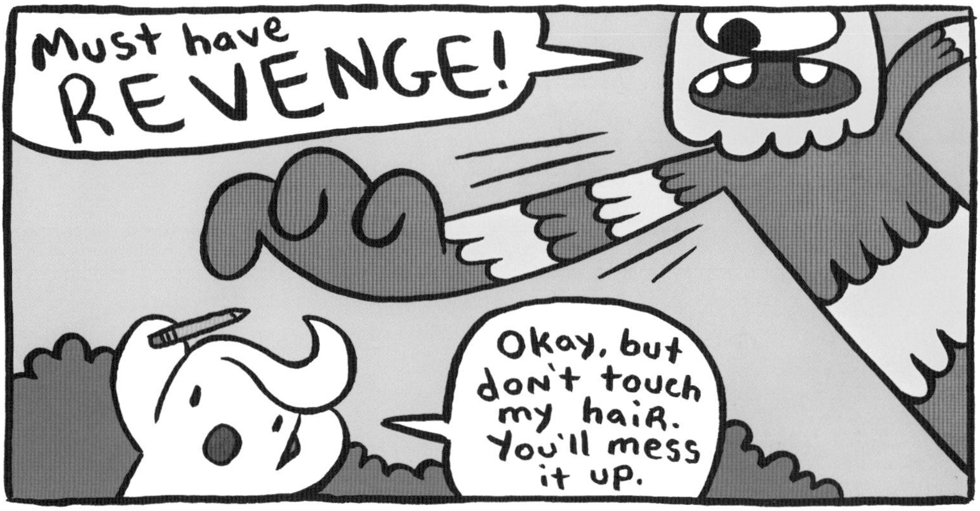
Must have REVENGE!
Okay, but don't touch my haiR. You'll mess it up.

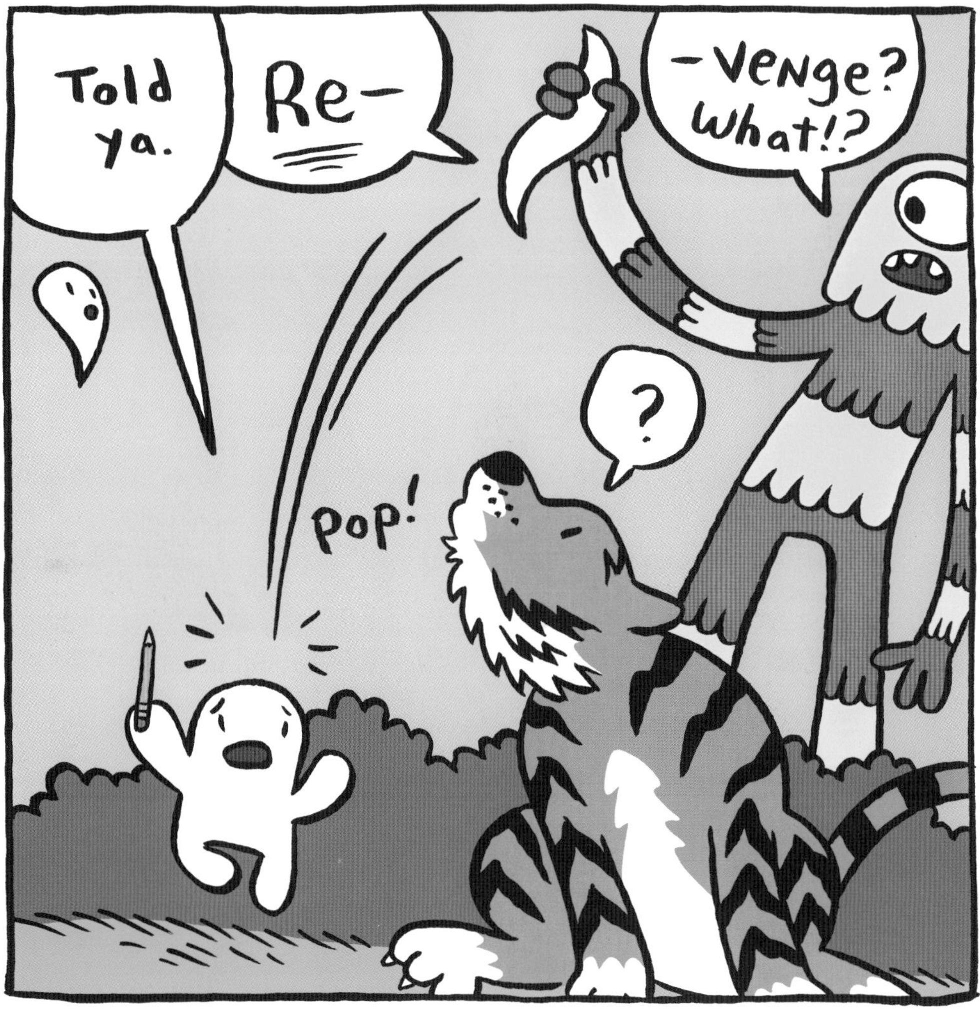
Told ya.
Re-
-venge? What!?
?
pop!

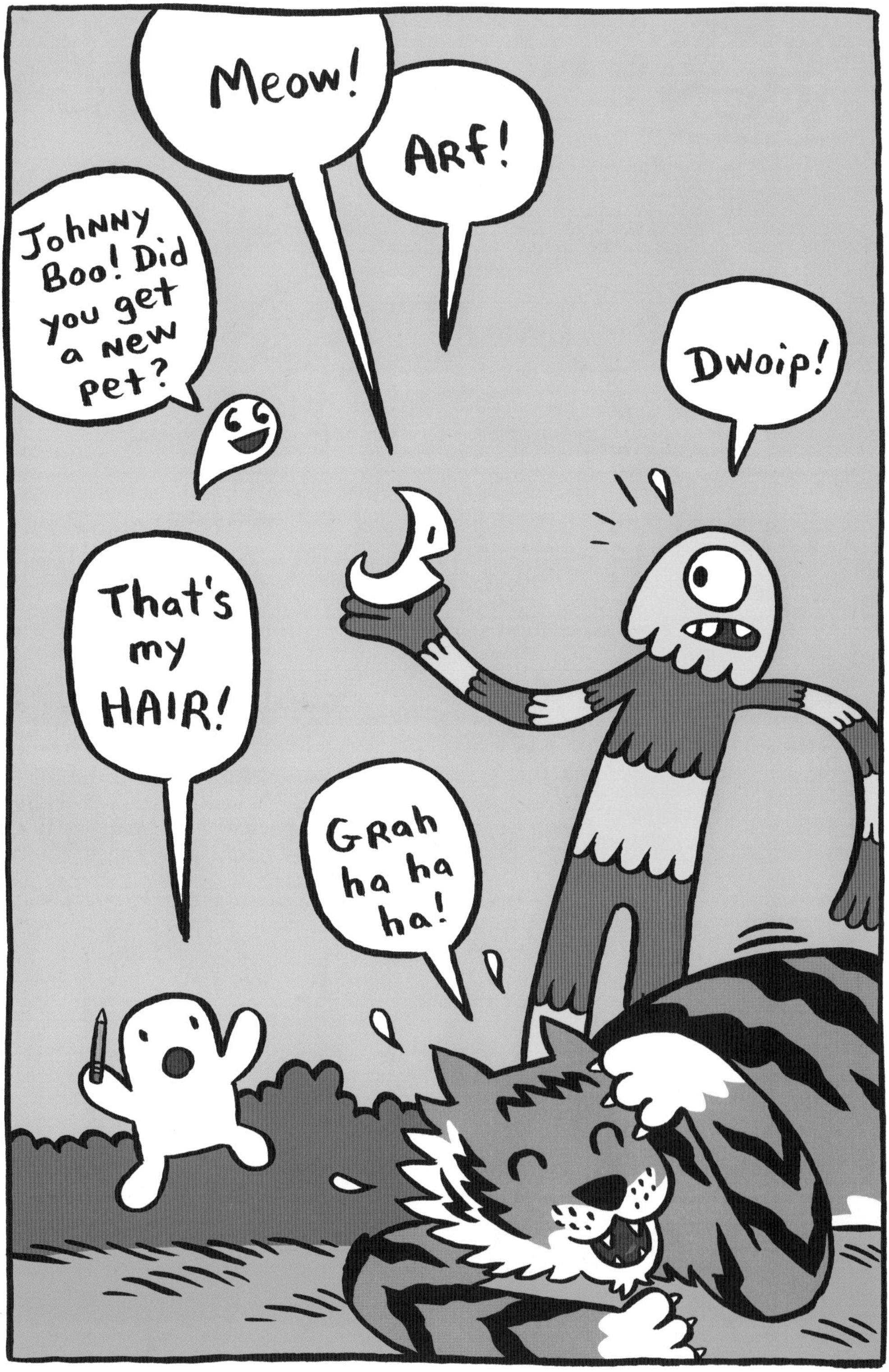
Meow!
ARf!
JohNNy Boo! Did you get a New pet?
Dwoip!
That's my HAIR!
GRah ha ha ha!

CHAPTER FOUR

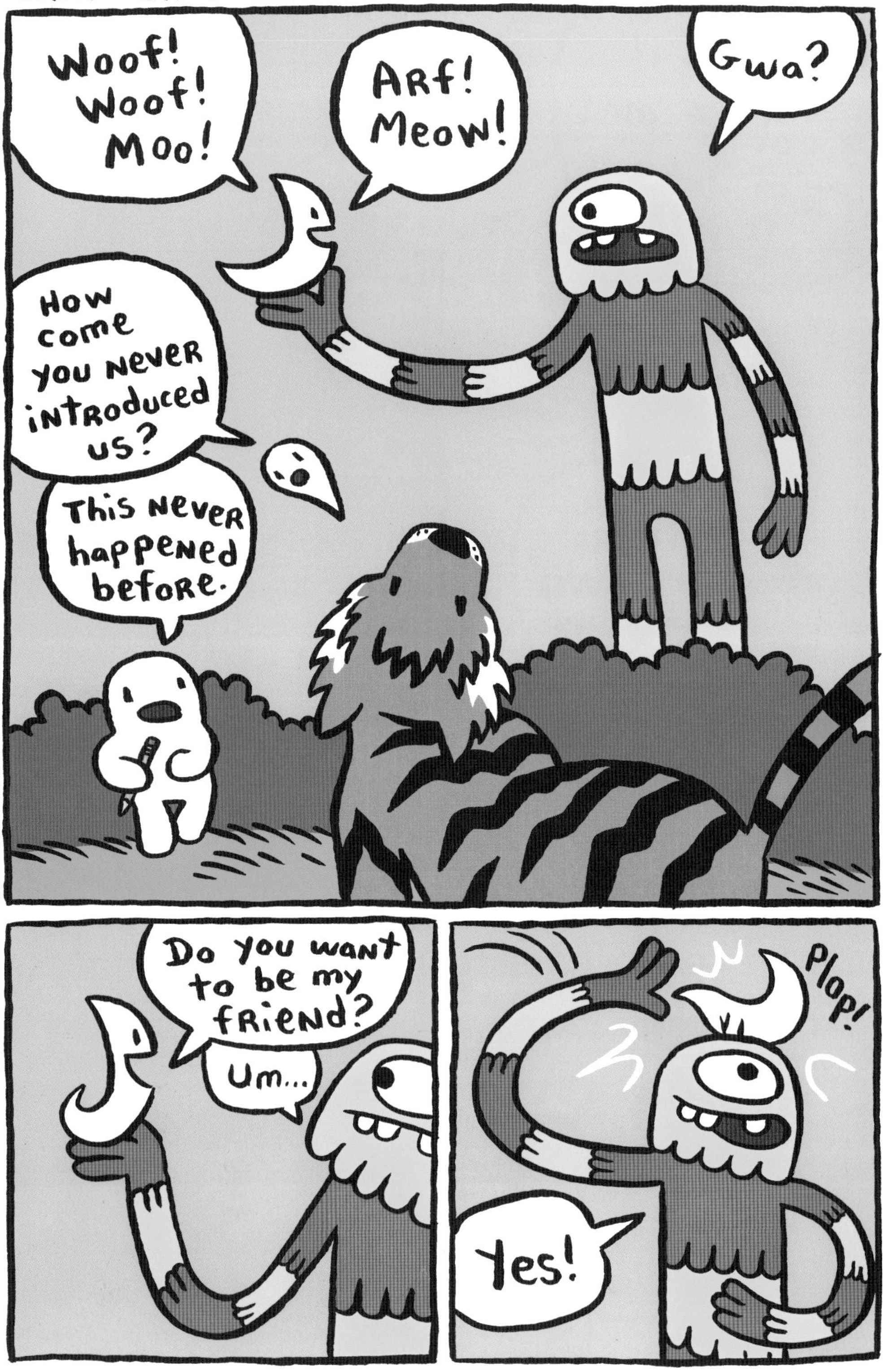
Woof! Woof! Moo!
Arf! Meow!
Gwa?
How come you never introduced us?
This never happened before.
Do you want to be my friend?
Um...
Plop!
Yes!

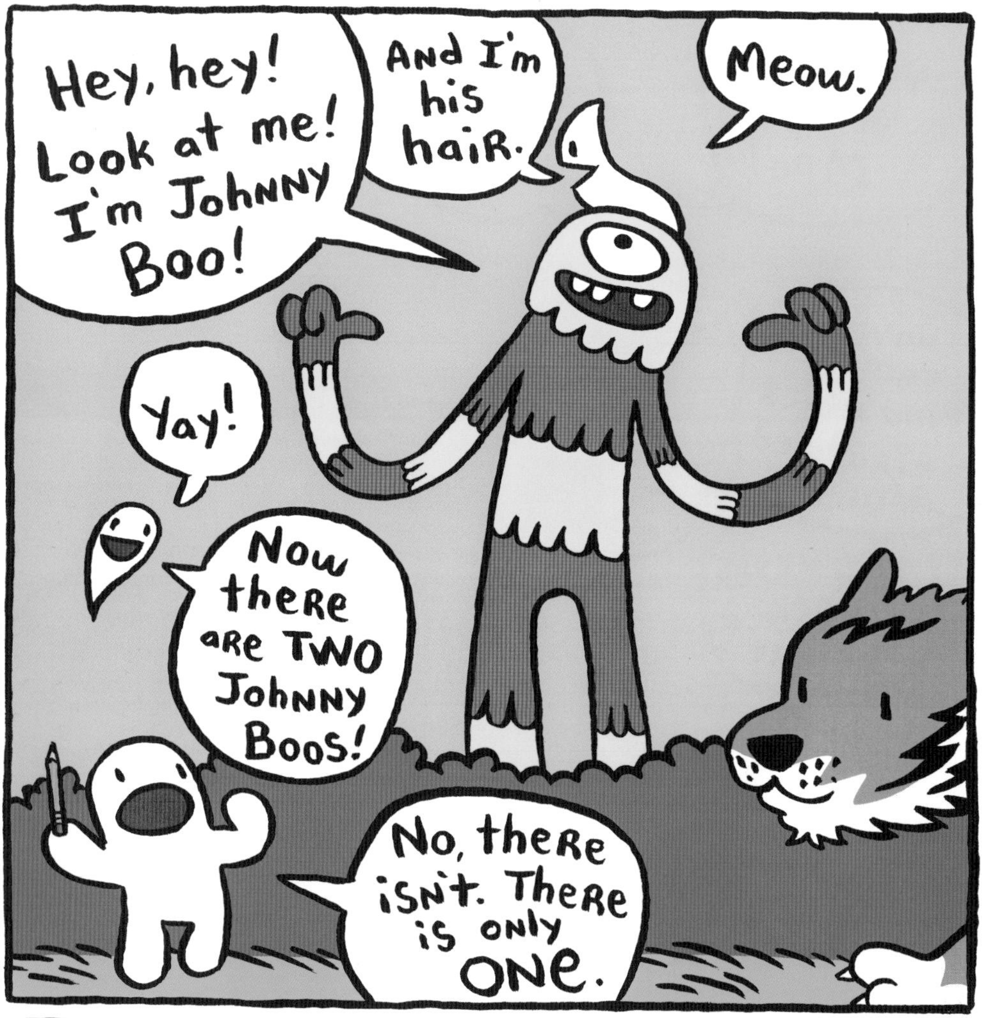
Hey, hey! Look at me! I'm Johnny Boo!
And I'm his hair.
Meow.
Yay!
Now there are TWO Johnny Boos!
No, there isn't. There is only ONE.

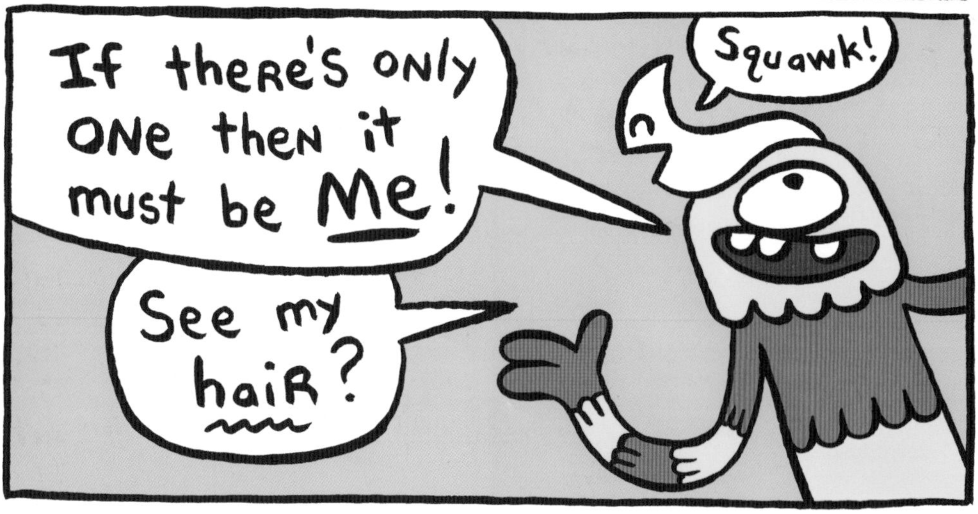
If there's only ONE then it must be Me!
Squawk!
See my hair?

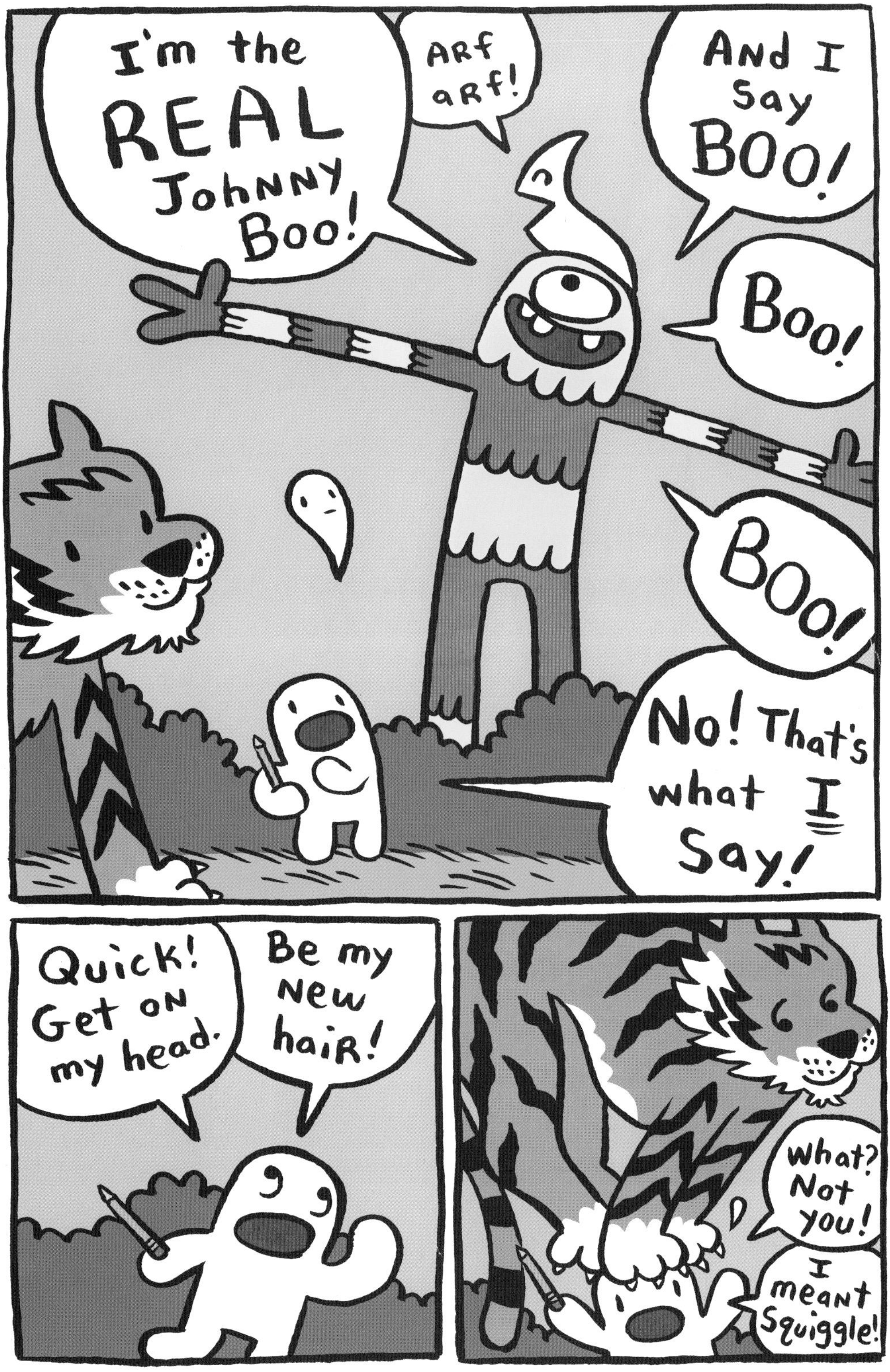
I'm the REAL Johnny Boo!
Arf arf!
And I say BOO!
Boo!
BOO!
No! That's what I say!
Quick! Get on my head.
Be my new hair!
What? Not you!
I meant Squiggle!

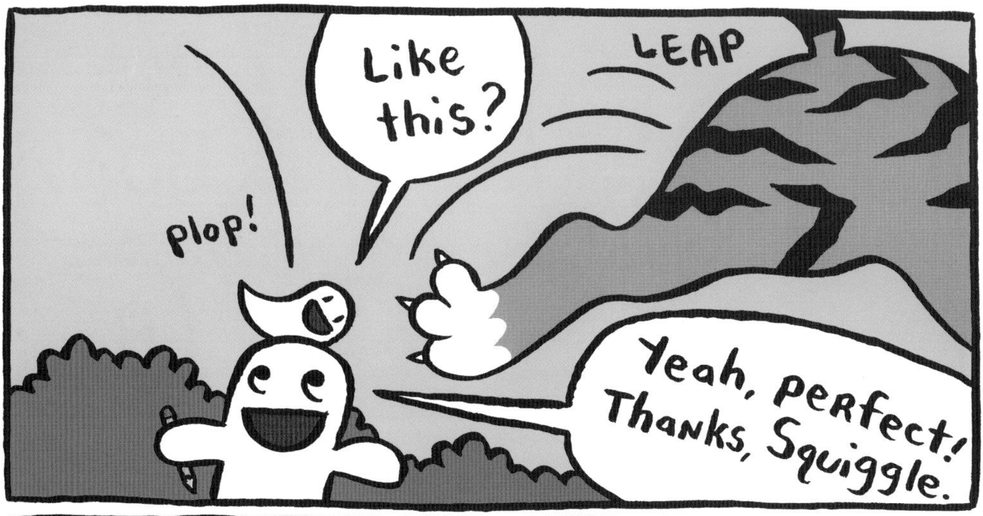
Like this?
LEAP
plop!
Yeah, perfect! Thanks, Squiggle.

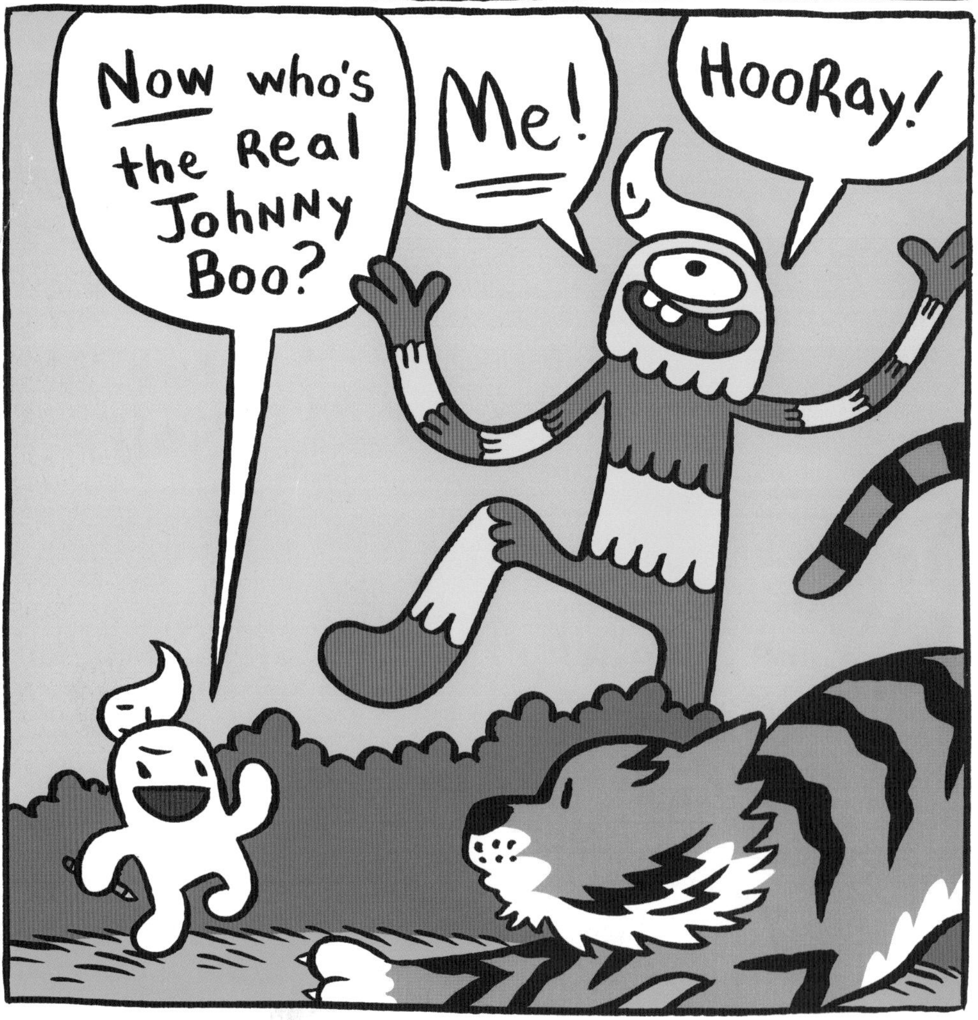
Now who's the real Johnny Boo?
Me!
Hooray!

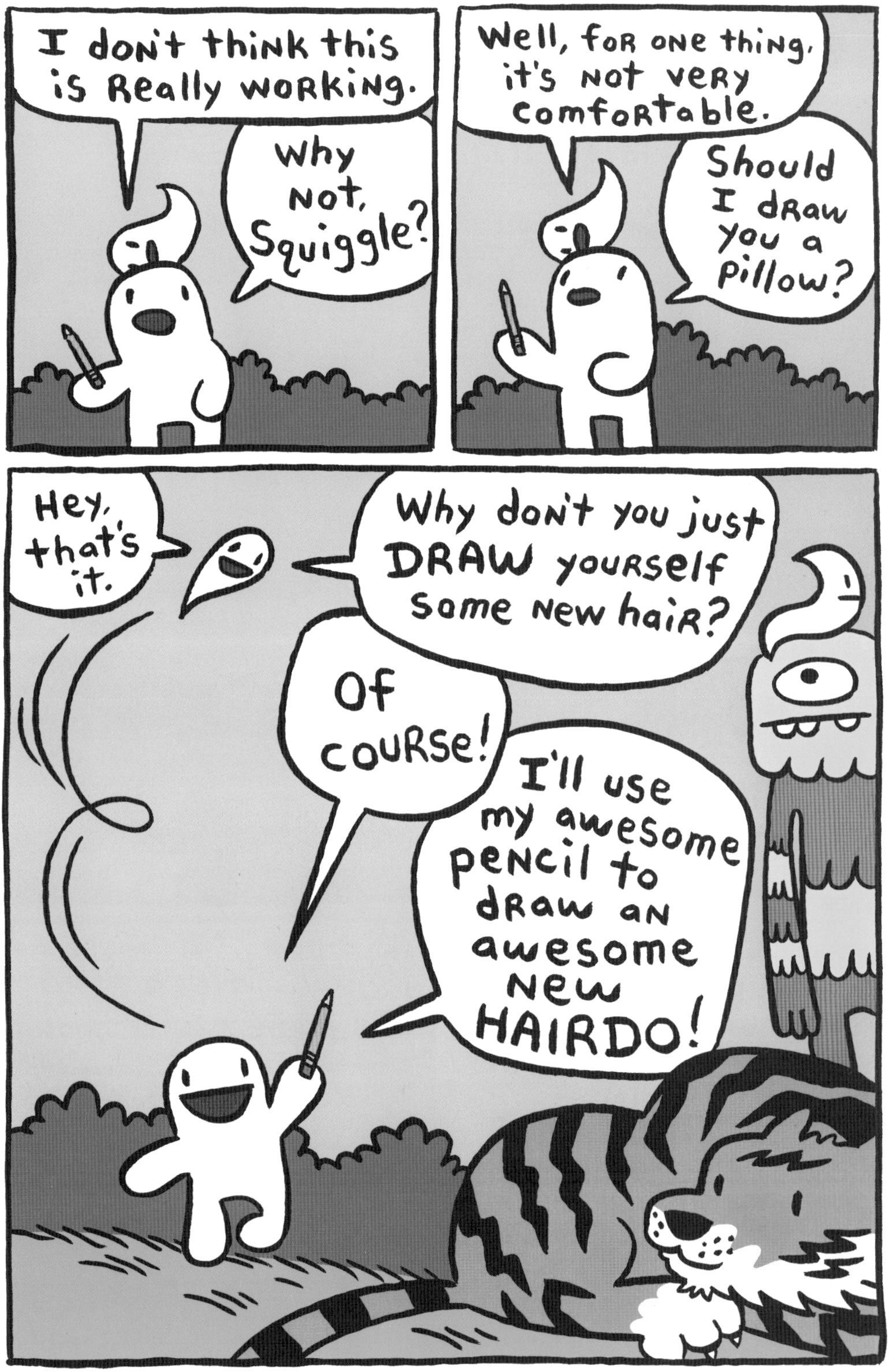
I don't think this is Really working.
Why not, Squiggle?
Well, for one thing, it's not very comfortable.
Should I draw you a pillow?
Hey, that's it.
Why don't you just DRAW yourself some new hair?
Of course!
I'll use my awesome pencil to draw an awesome new HAIRDO!

CHAPTER FIVE

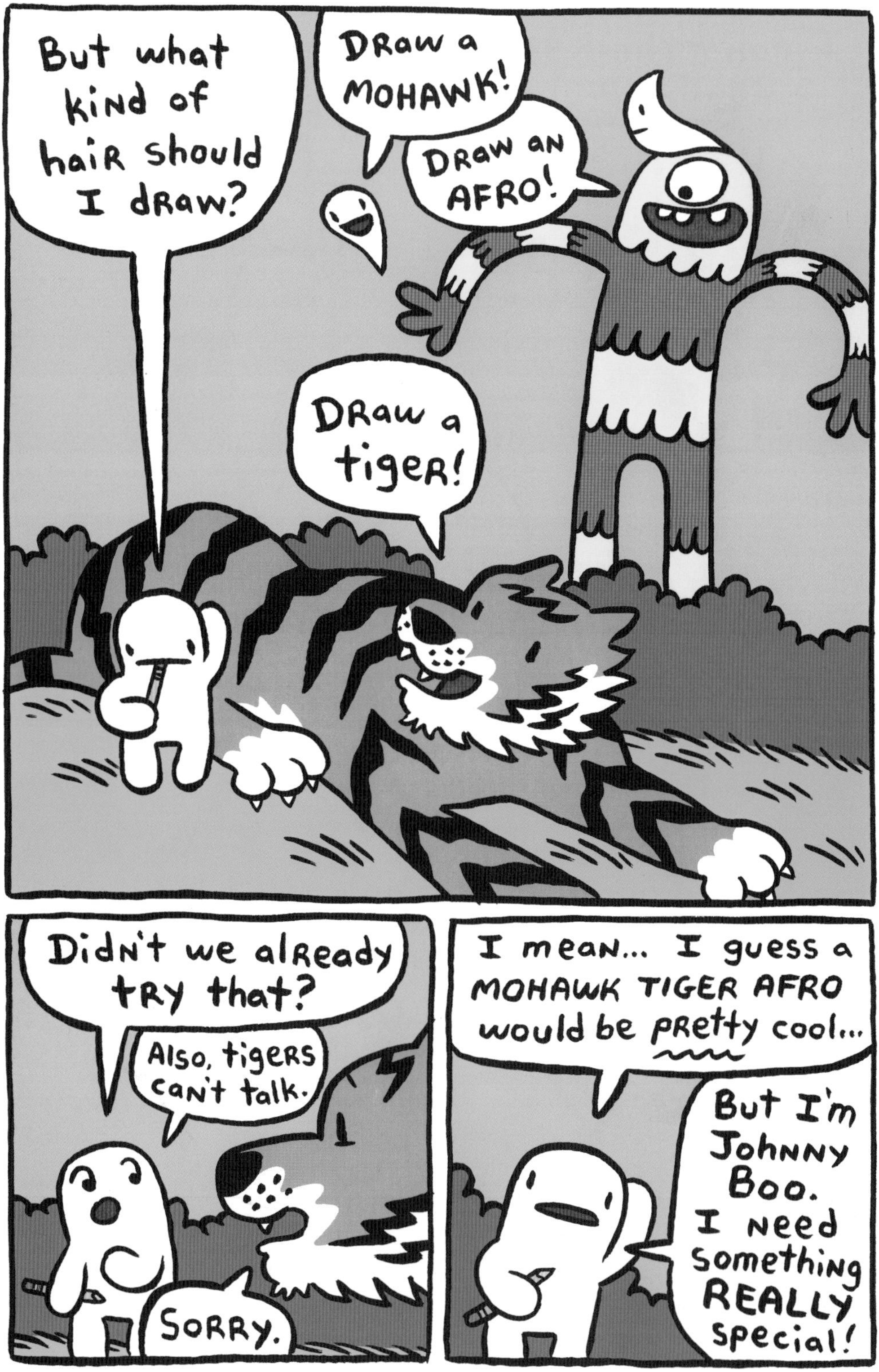

But what kind of hair should I draw?
Draw a MOHAWK!
Draw an AFRO!
Draw a tiger!
Didn't we already try that?
Also, tigers can't talk.
Sorry.
I mean... I guess a MOHAWK TIGER AFRO would be pretty cool...
But I'm Johnny Boo. I need something REALLY special!

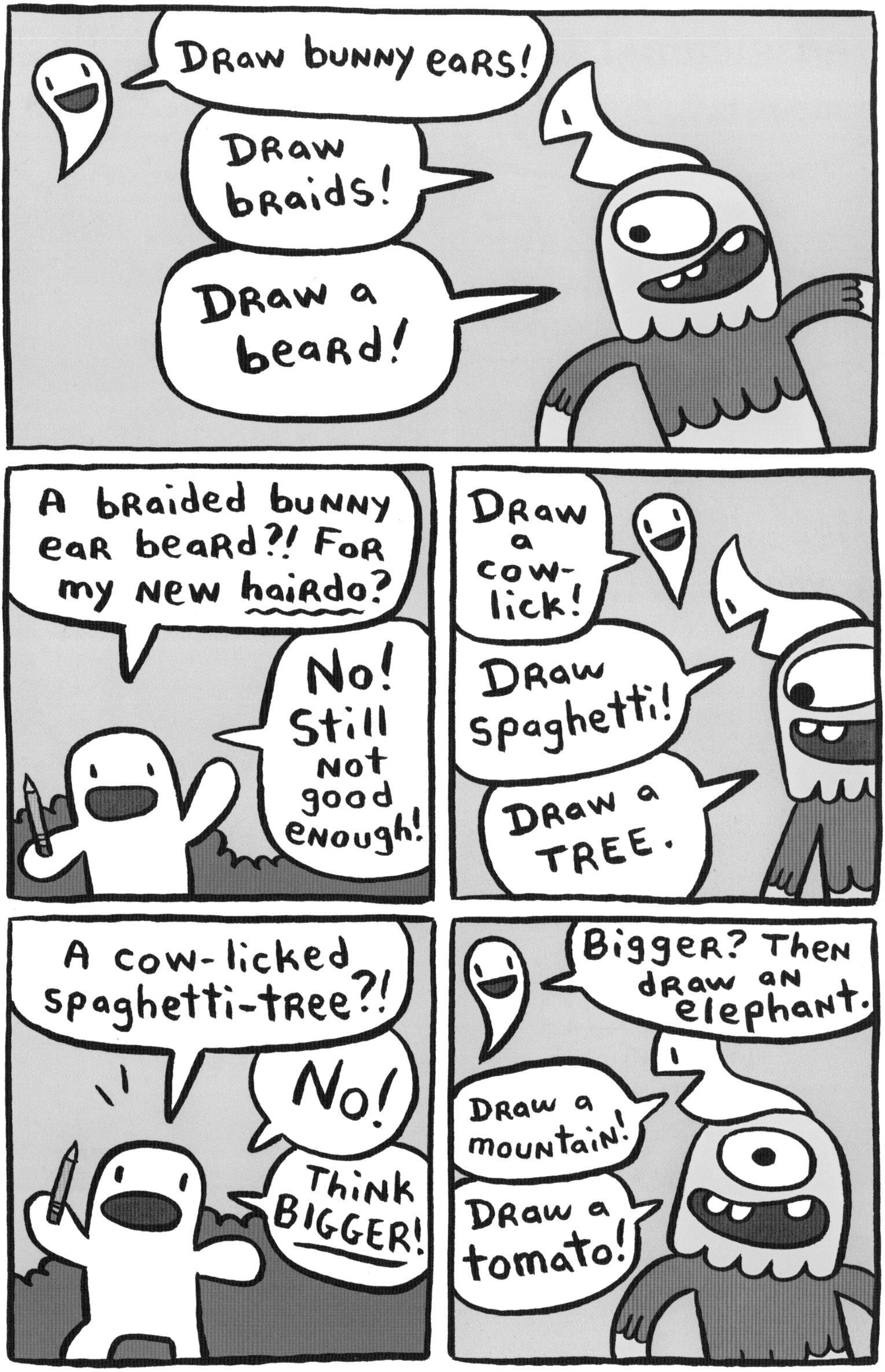
Draw bunny ears!
Draw braids!
Draw a beard!
A braided bunny ear beard?! For my new hairdo?
No! Still not good enough!
Draw a cow-lick!
Draw spaghetti!
Draw a TREE.
A cow-licked spaghetti-tree?!
No!
Think BIGGER!
Bigger? Then draw an elephant.
Draw a mountain!
Draw a tomato!

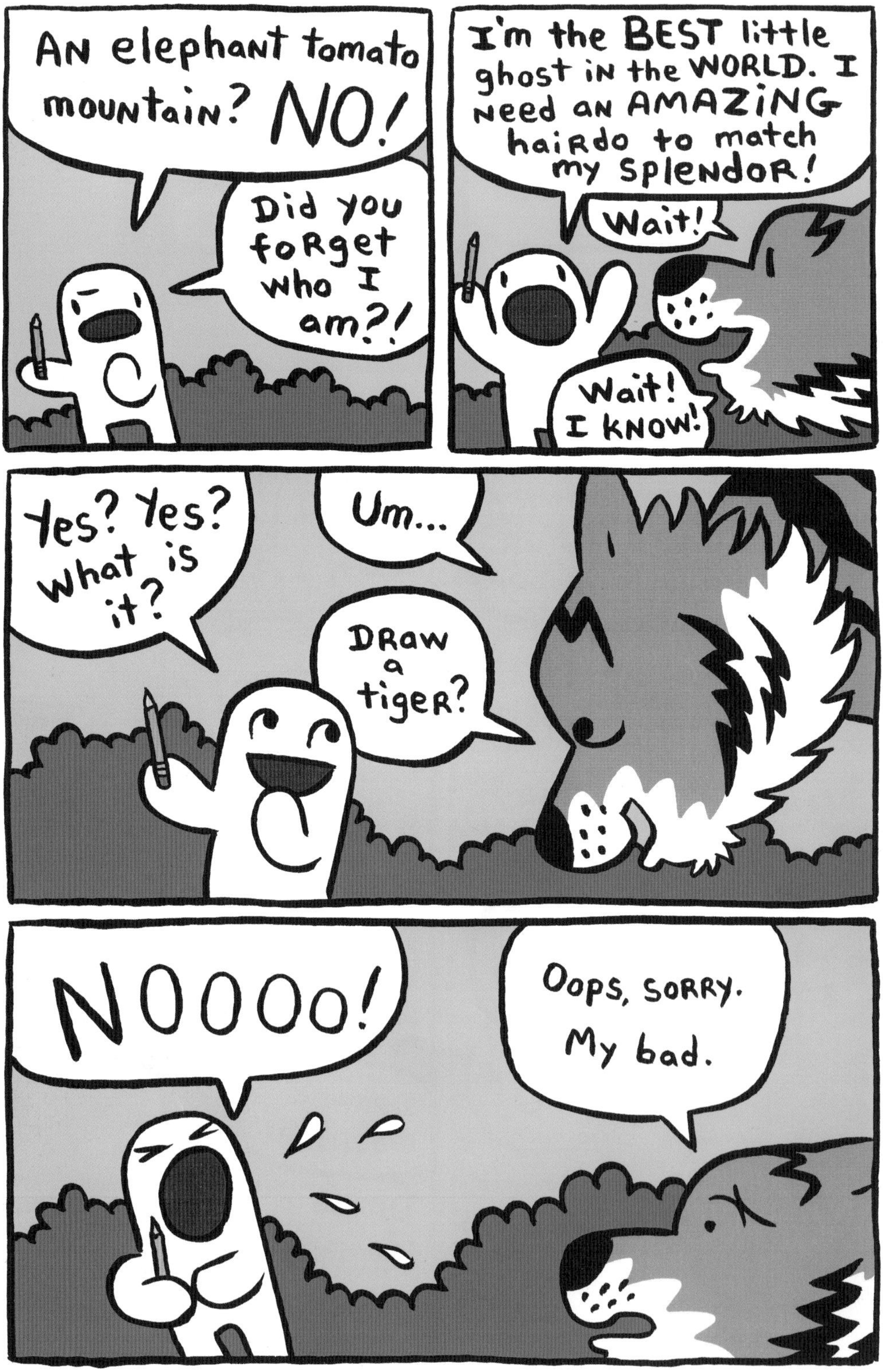
An elephant tomato mountain? NO!
Did you forget who I am?!
I'm the BEST little ghost in the WORLD. I need an AMAZING hairdo to match my splendor!
Wait!
Wait! I know!
Yes? Yes? What is it?
Um...
Draw a tiger?
Noooo!
Oops, sorry.
My bad.

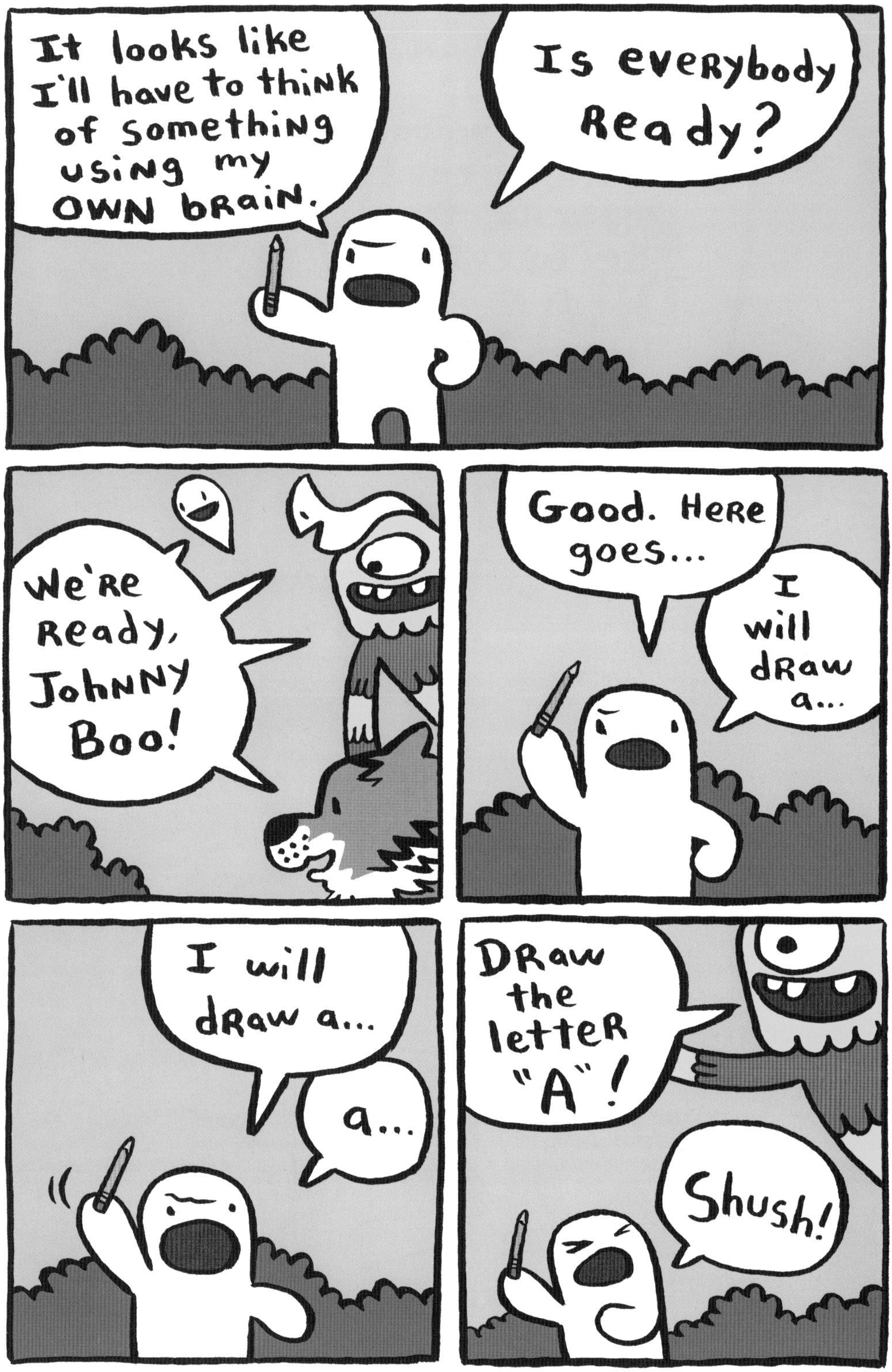
It looks like I'll have to think of something using my OWN brain.
Is everybody Ready?
We're Ready, Johnny Boo!
Good. Here goes...
I will draw a...
I will draw a...
a...
Draw the letter "A"!
Shush!

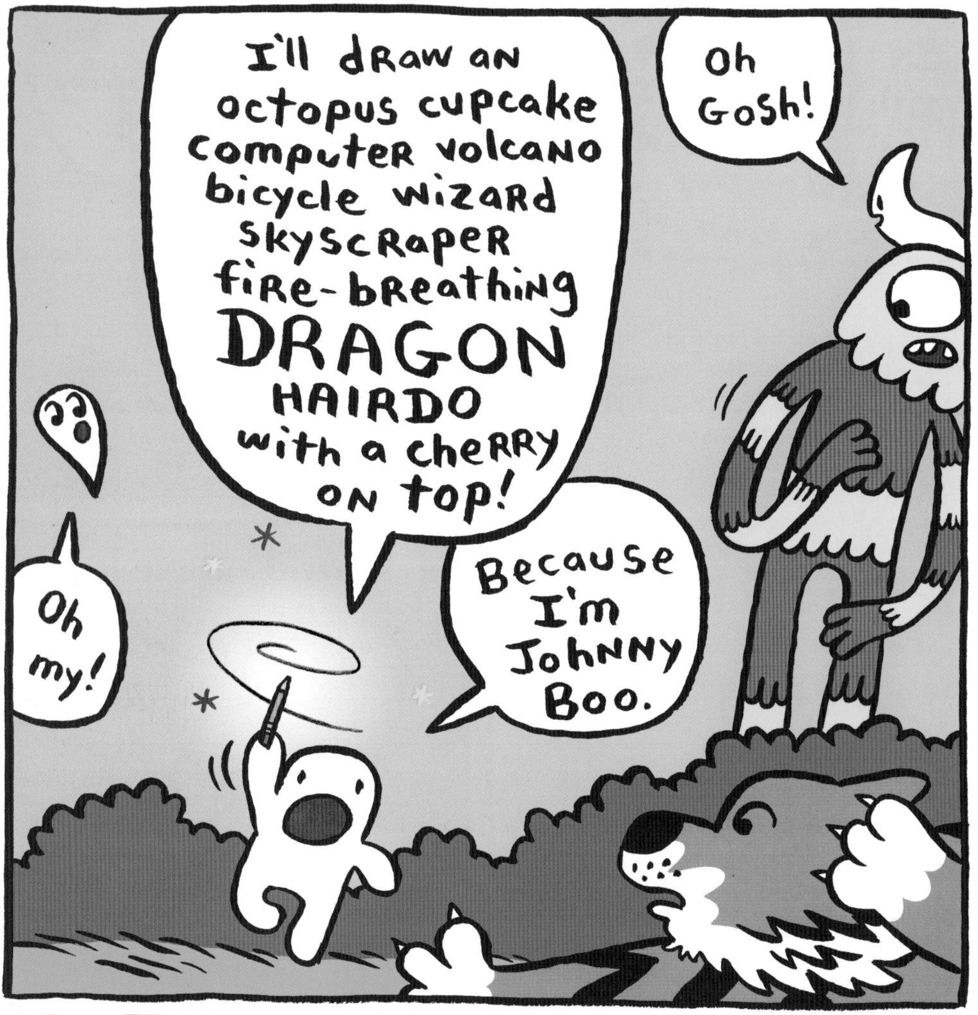
I'll draw an octopus cupcake computer volcano bicycle wizard skyscraper fire-breathing DRAGON HAIRDO with a cherry on top!
Oh Gosh!
Oh my!
Because I'm Johnny Boo.

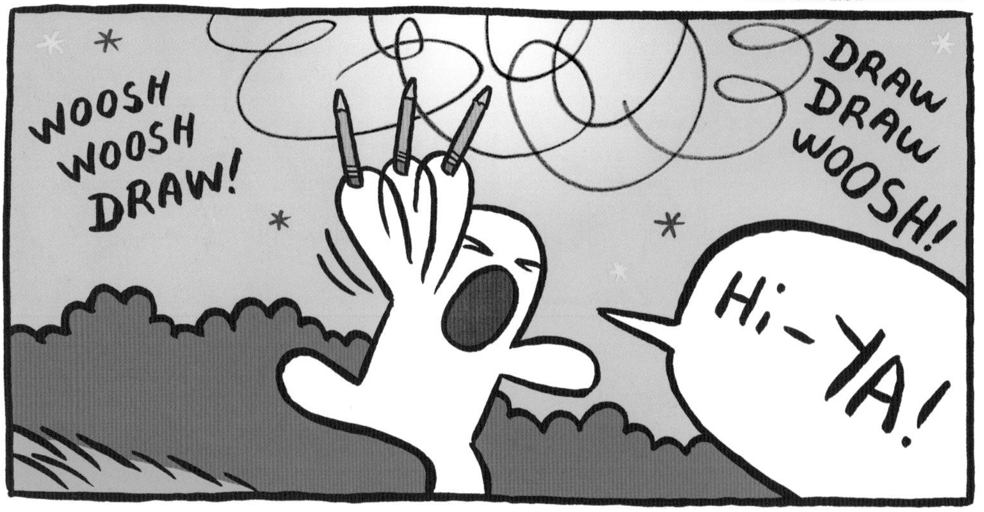
WOOSH WOOSH DRAW!
DRAW DRAW WOOSH!
Hi-YA!

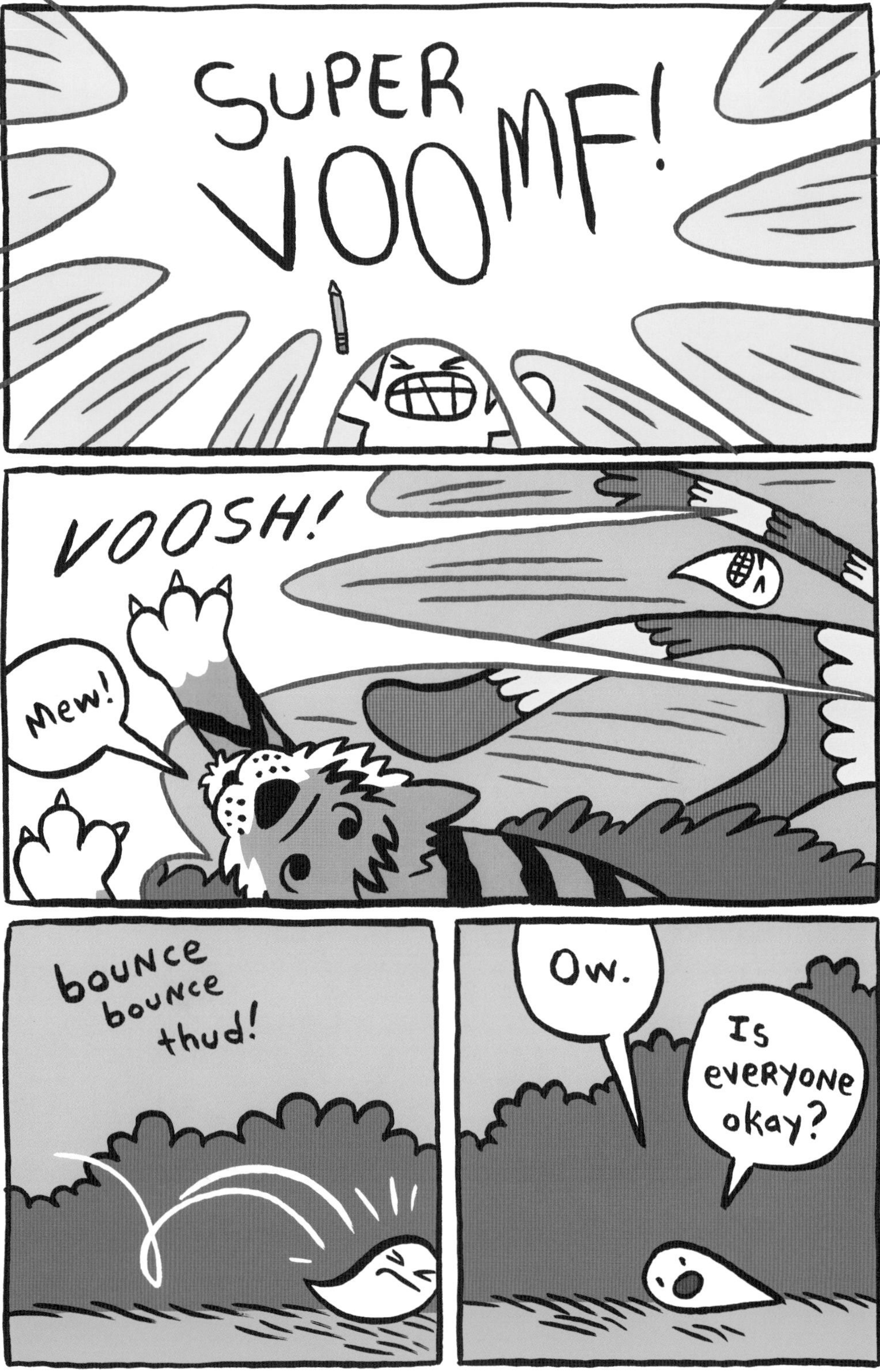
SUPER VOOMF!
VOOSH!
Mew!
bounce bounce thud!
Ow.
Is everyone okay?

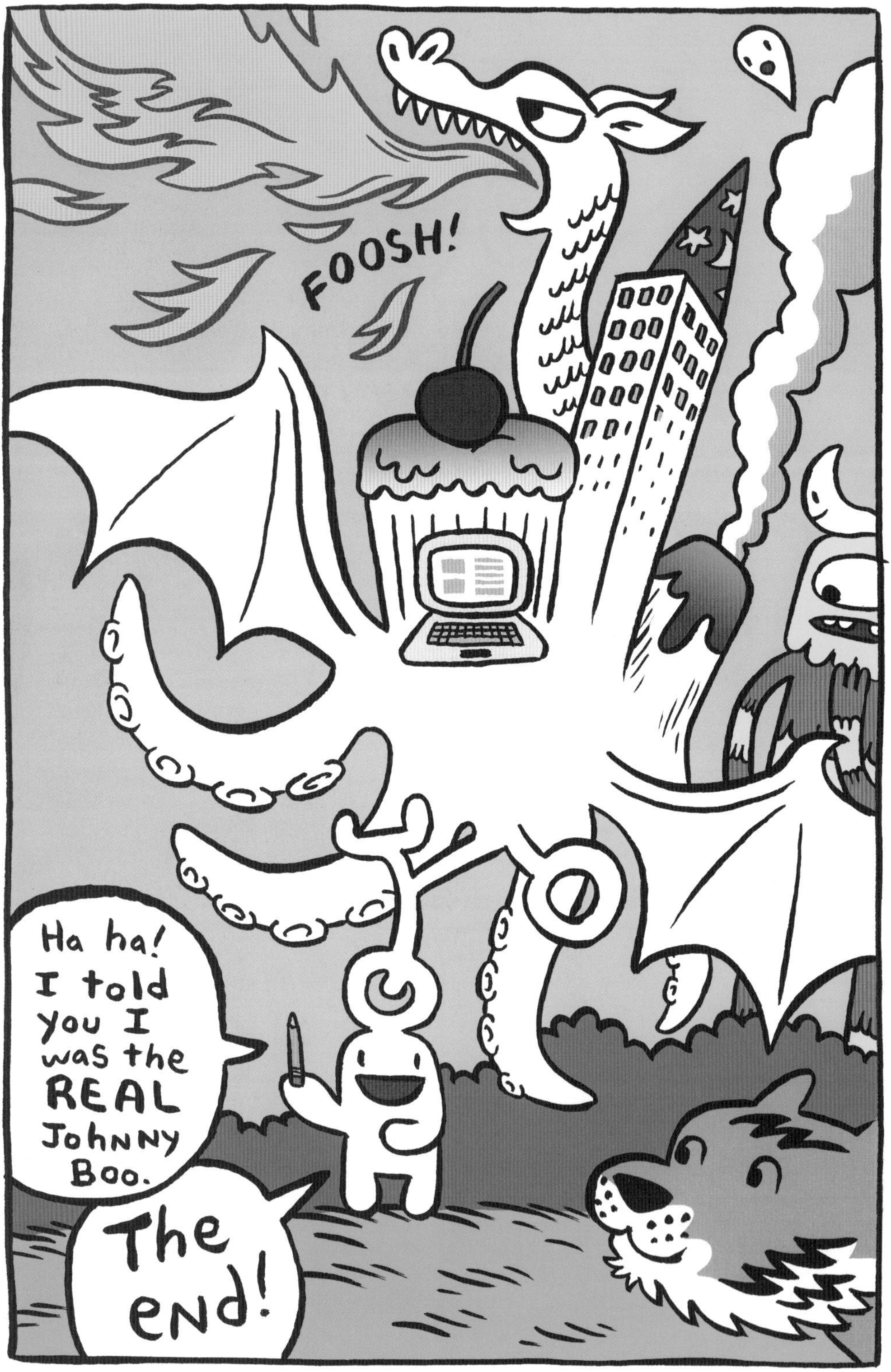
FOOSH!
Ha ha! I told you I was the REAL Johnny Boo.
The end!

CHAPTER SIX

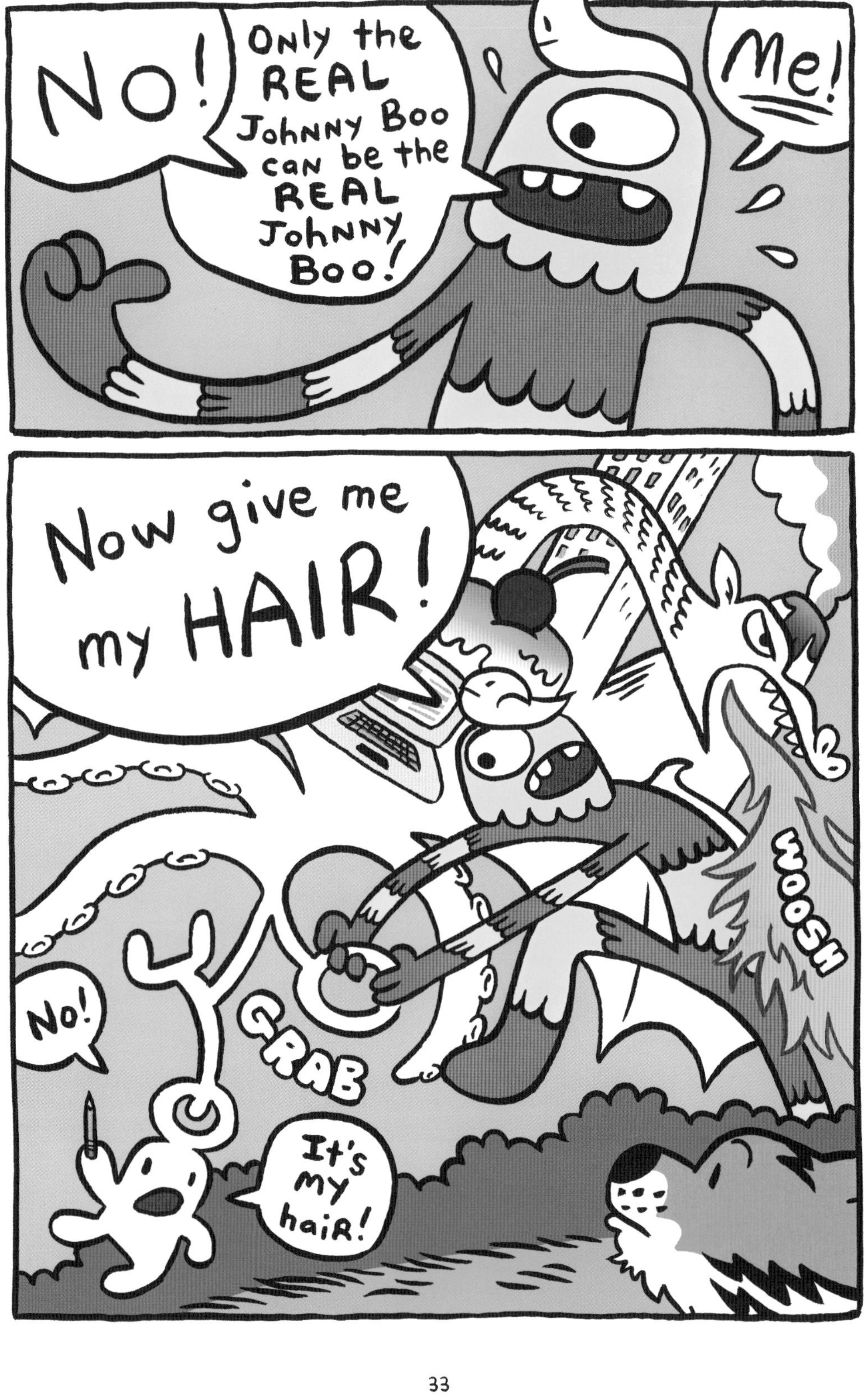
NO!
Only the REAL Johnny Boo can be the REAL Johnny Boo!
Me!
Now give me my HAIR!
WOOSH
No!
GRAB
It's my hair!

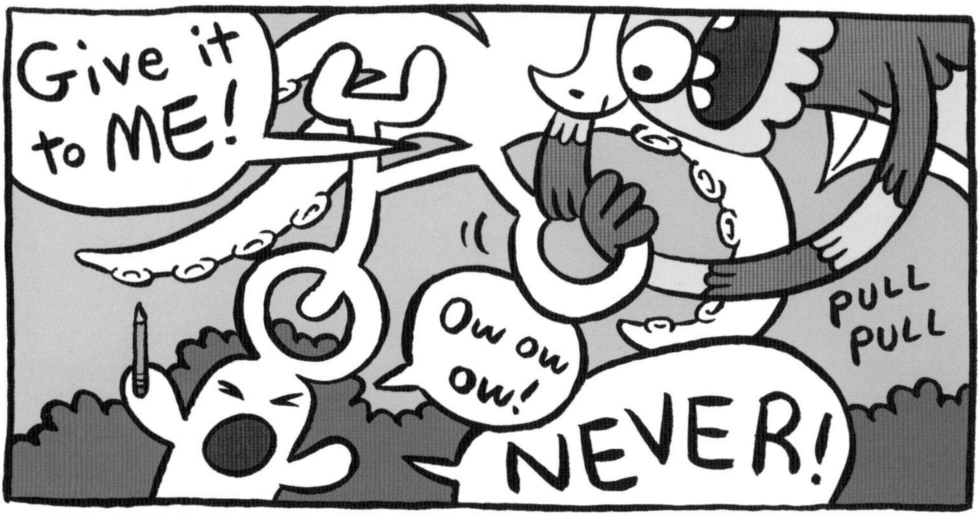
Give it to ME!
Ow ow ow!
NEVER!
PULL PULL

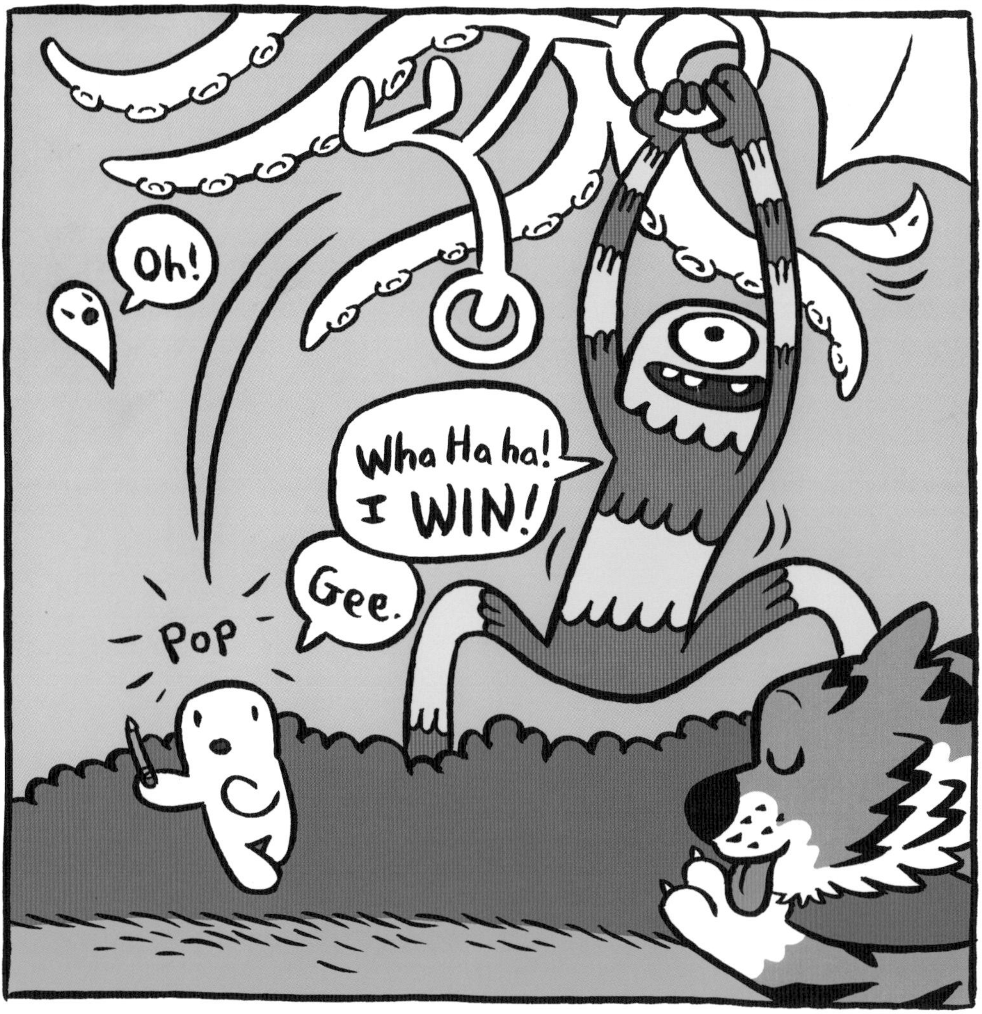
Oh!
Wha Ha ha! I WIN!
Gee.
Pop

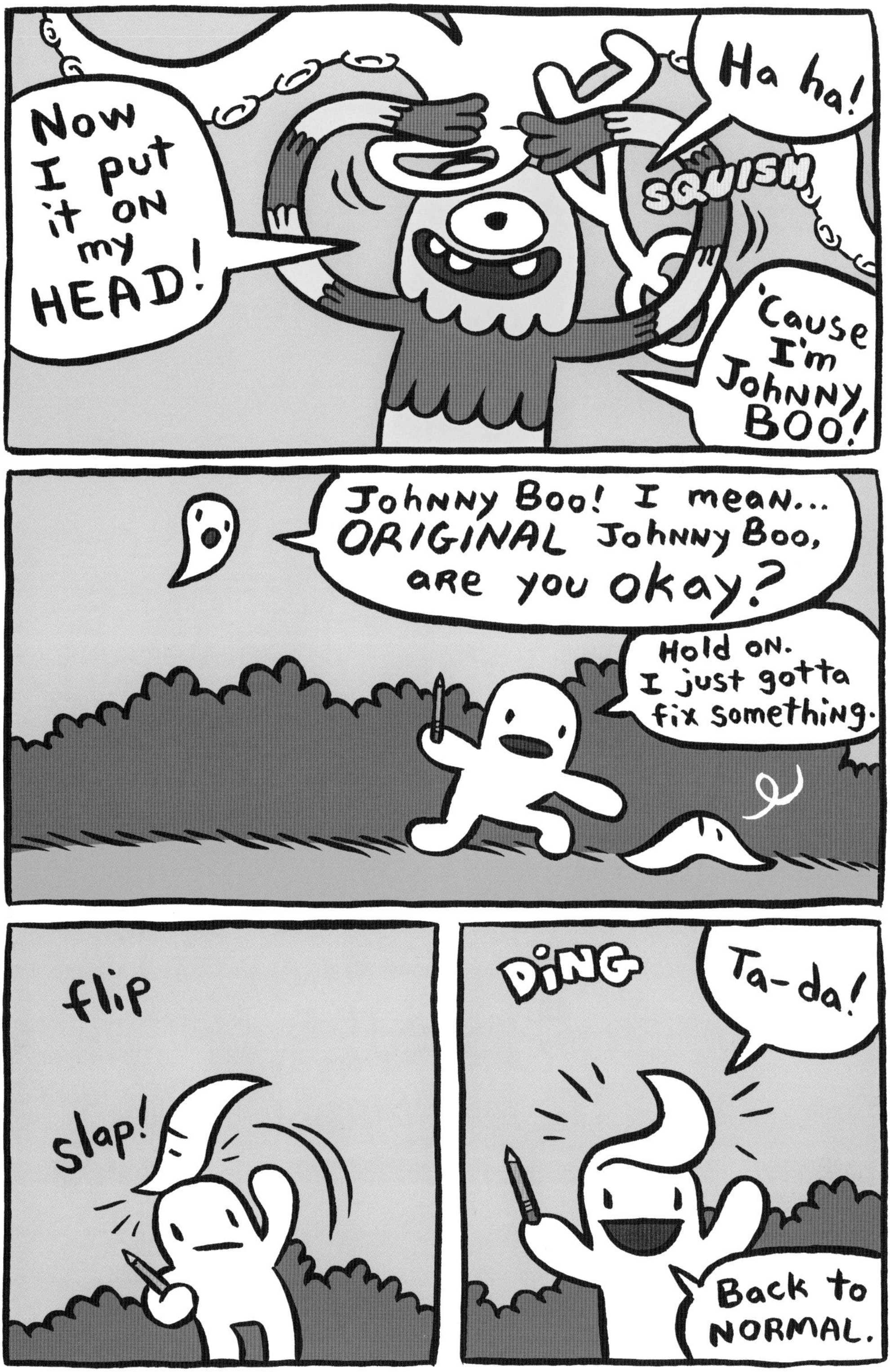
Now I put it ON my HEAD!
Ha ha!
SQUISH
'Cause I'm Johnny BOO!
Johnny Boo! I mean... ORIGINAL Johnny Boo, are you okay?
Hold on. I just gotta fix something.
flip
slap!
DING
Ta-da!
Back to NORMAL.

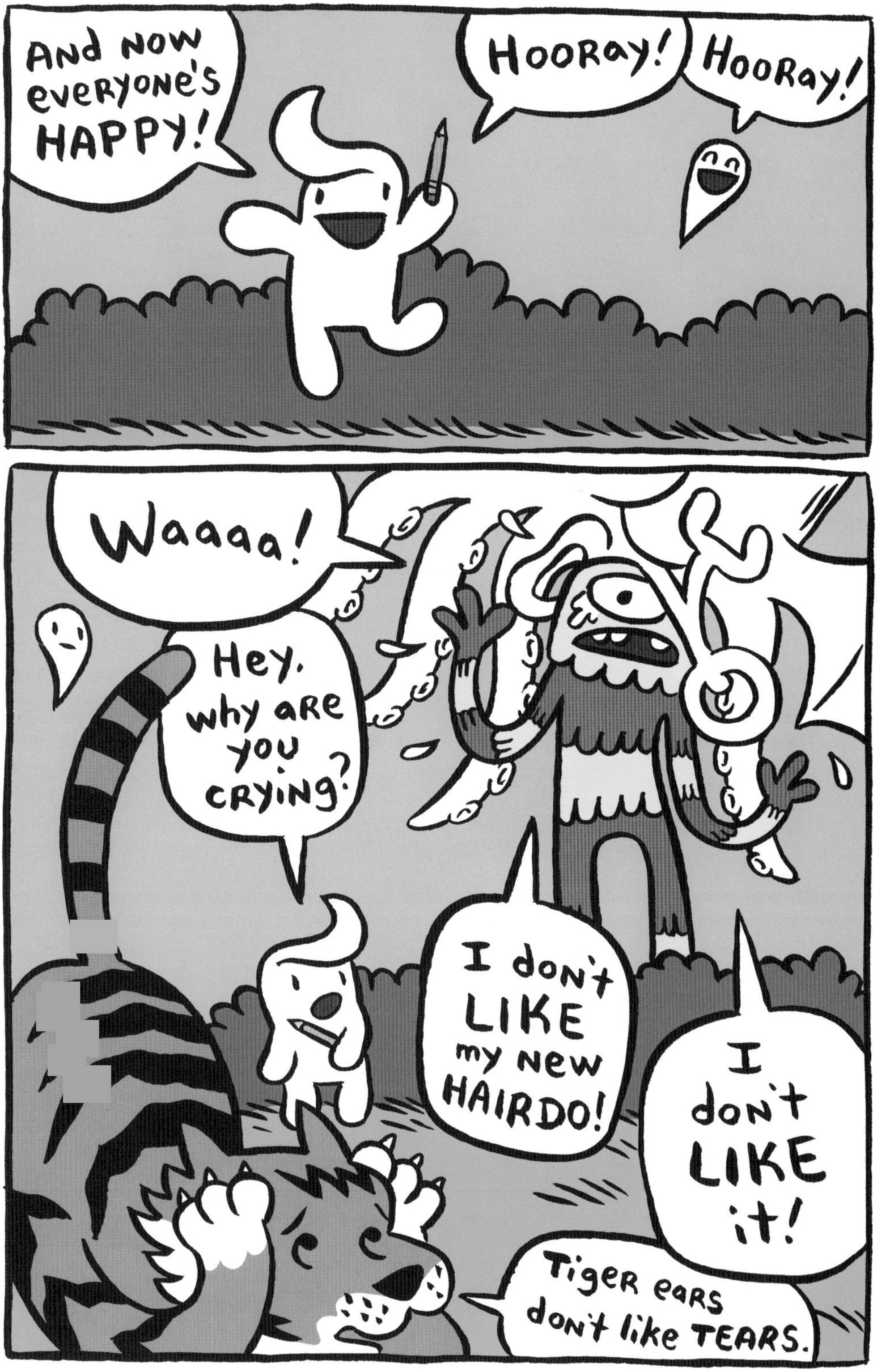
And now everyone's HAPPY!
Hooray!
Hooray!
Waaaa!
Hey, why are you crying?
I don't LIKE my new HAIRDO!
I don't LIKE it!
Tiger ears don't like TEARS.

CHAPTER SEVEN

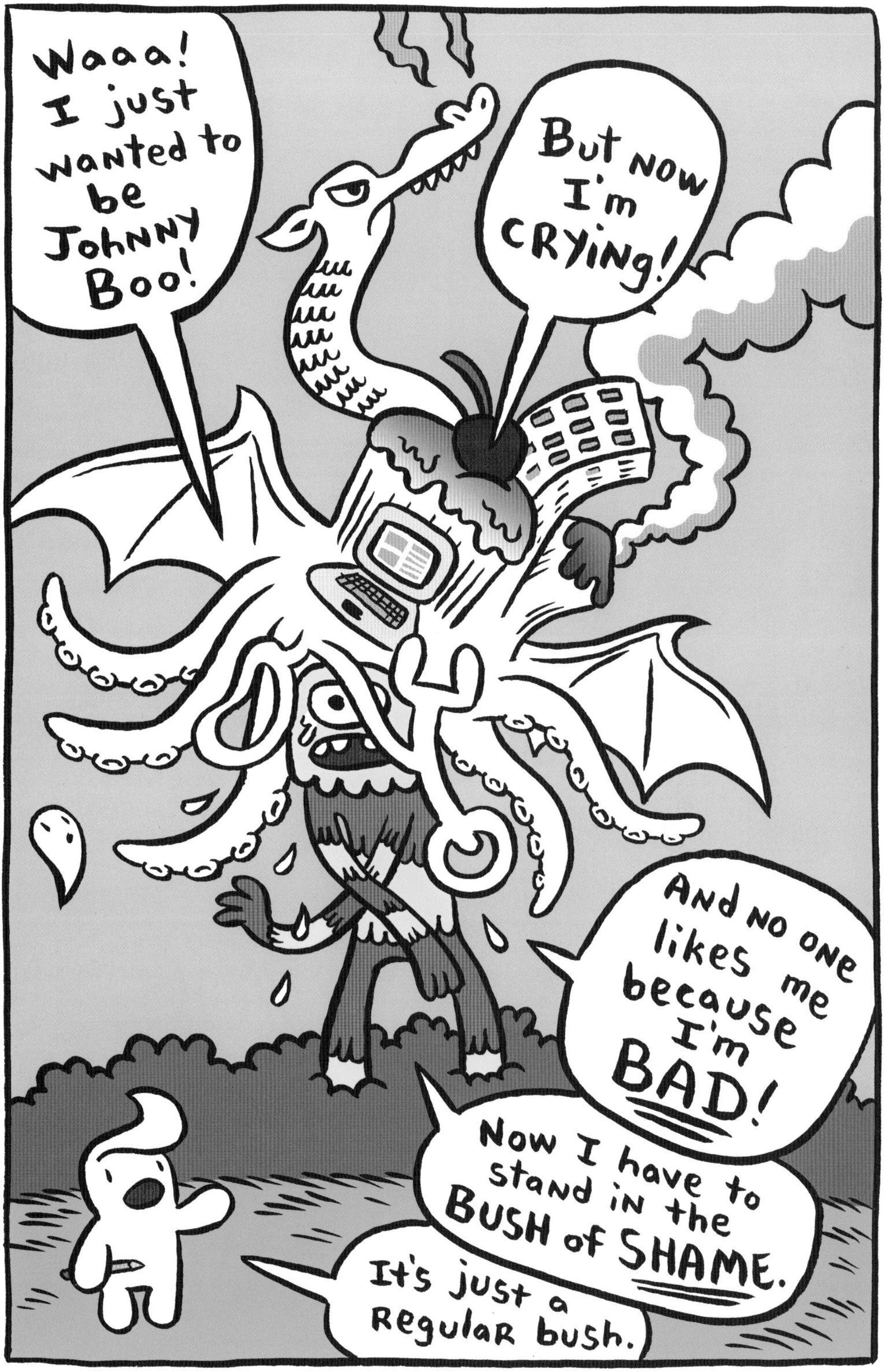
Waaa! I just wanted to be Johnny Boo!
But now I'm CRYING!
And no one likes me because I'm BAD!
Now I have to stand in the BUSH of SHAME.
It's just a regular bush.

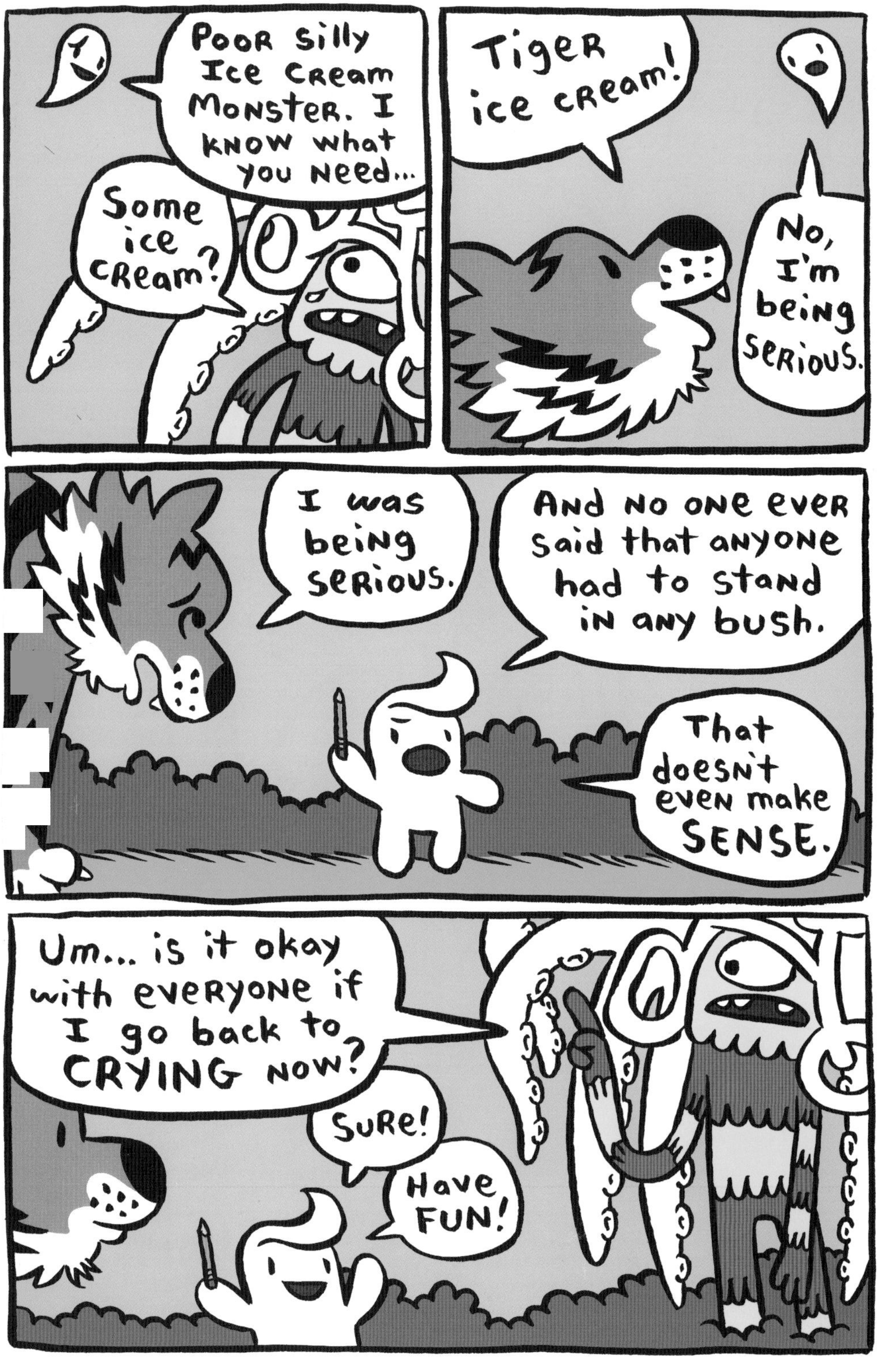
Poor silly Ice Cream Monster. I know what you need...
Some ice cream?
Tiger ice cream!
No, I'm being serious.
I was being serious.
And no one ever said that anyone had to stand in any bush.
That doesn't even make SENSE.
Um... is it okay with everyone if I go back to CRYING now?
Sure!
Have FUN!

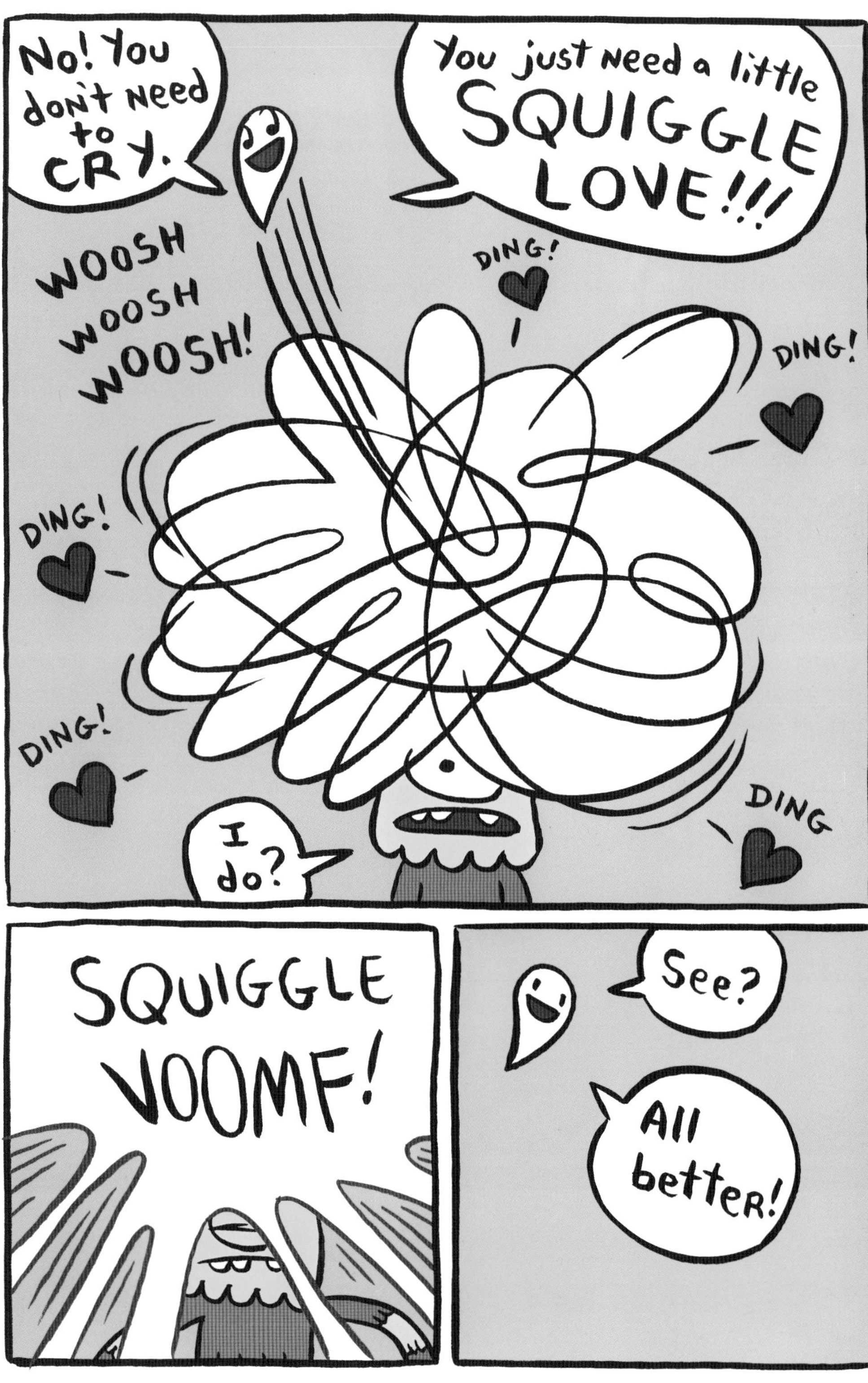
No! You don't need to CRY.
You just need a little SQUIGGLE LOVE!!!
WOOSH WOOSH WOOSH!
DING!
DING!
DING!
DING!
I do?
DING
SQUIGGLE VOOMF!
See?
All better!

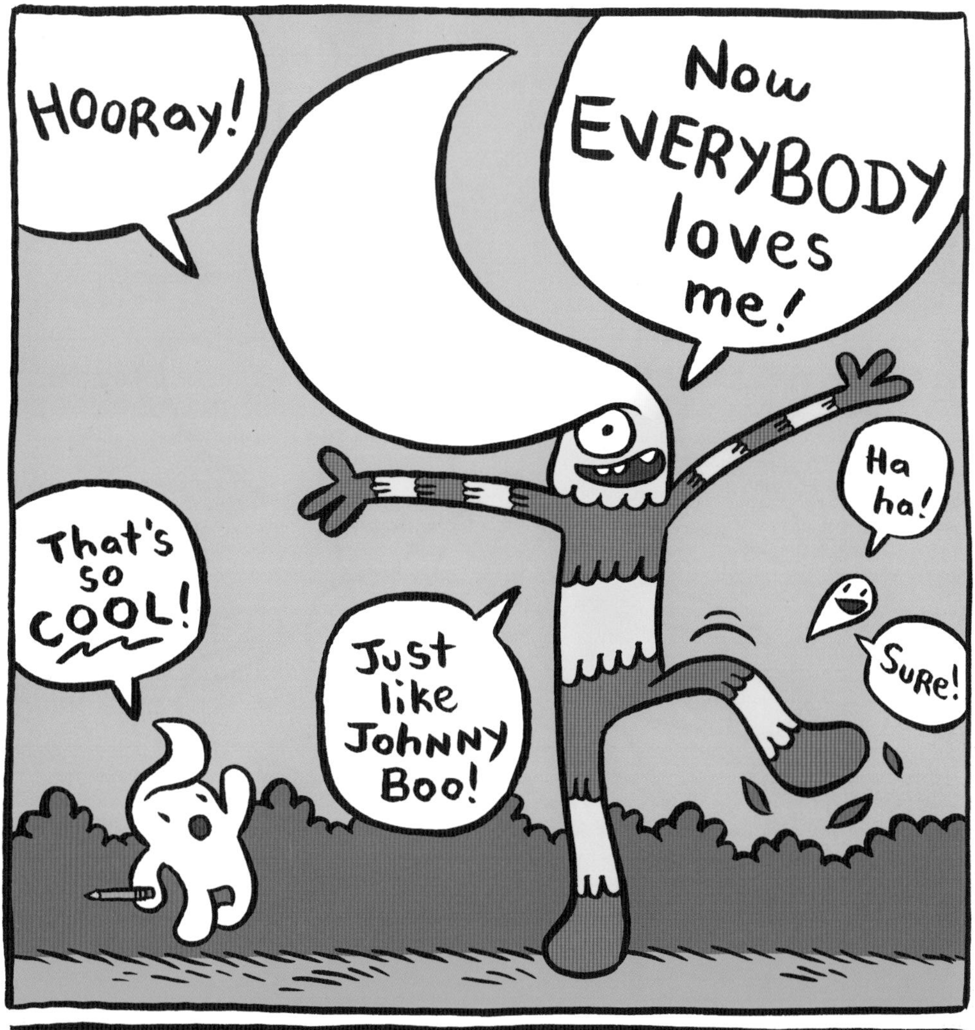
HOORAY!
Now EVERYBODY loves me!
That's so COOL!
Just like Johnny Boo!
Ha ha!
Sure!

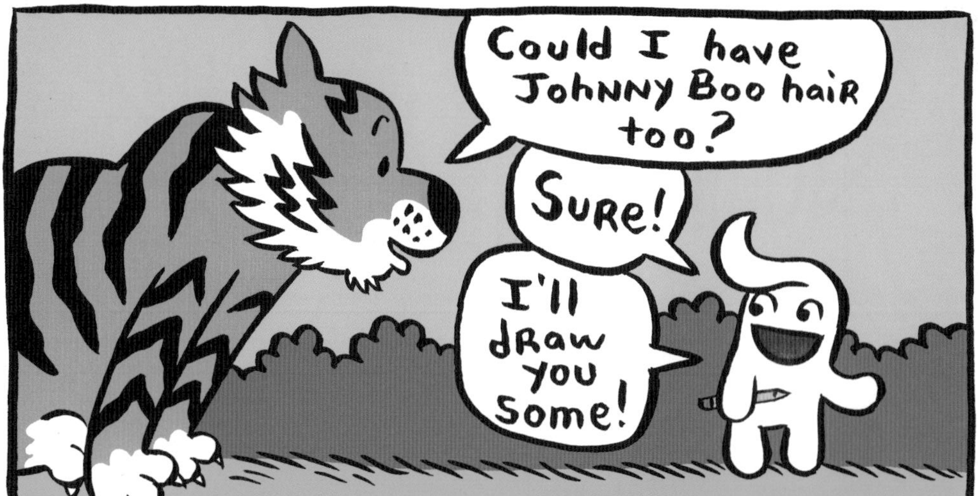
Could I have Johnny Boo hair too?
Sure!
I'll draw you some!

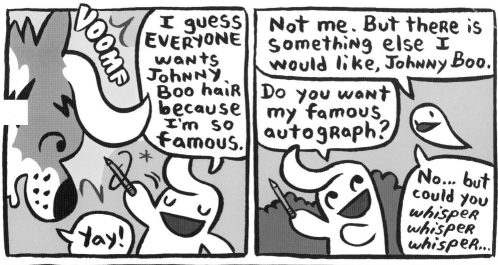

VOOMF

I guess EVERYONE wants JohnnY Boo haiR because I'm so famous.

Yay!

Not me. But there is something else I would like, Johnny Boo.

Do you want my famous autograph?

No... but could you whisper whisper whisper...

SURE!

I'd LOVE to dRaw that!

Is it a tiger?

Hold still, Squiggle. Here it comes!

DRAW DRAW

VOOMF

Ha ha!

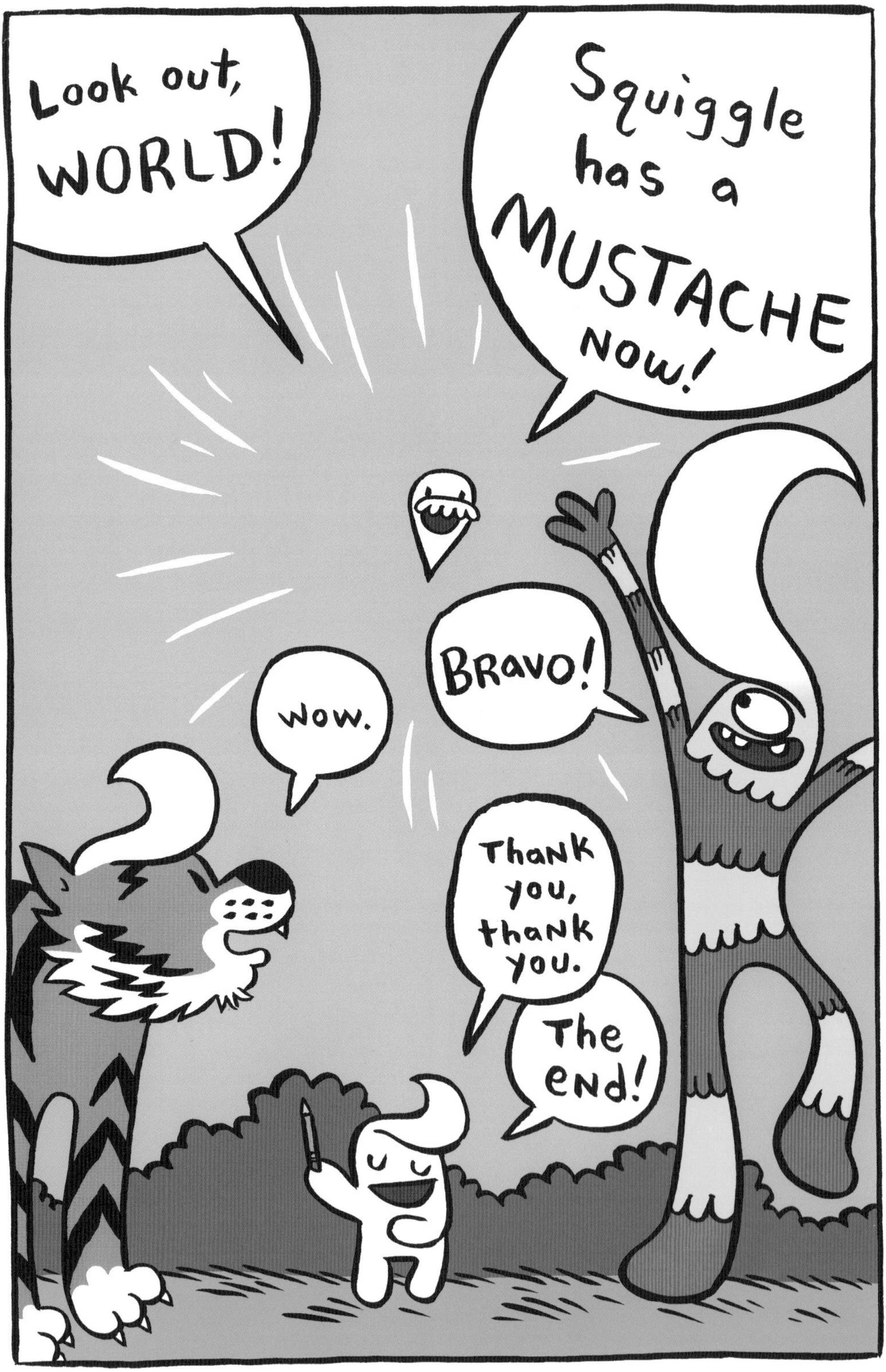
Look out, WORLD!
Squiggle has a MUSTACHE now!
BRAVO!
WOW.
Thank you, thank you.
The end!

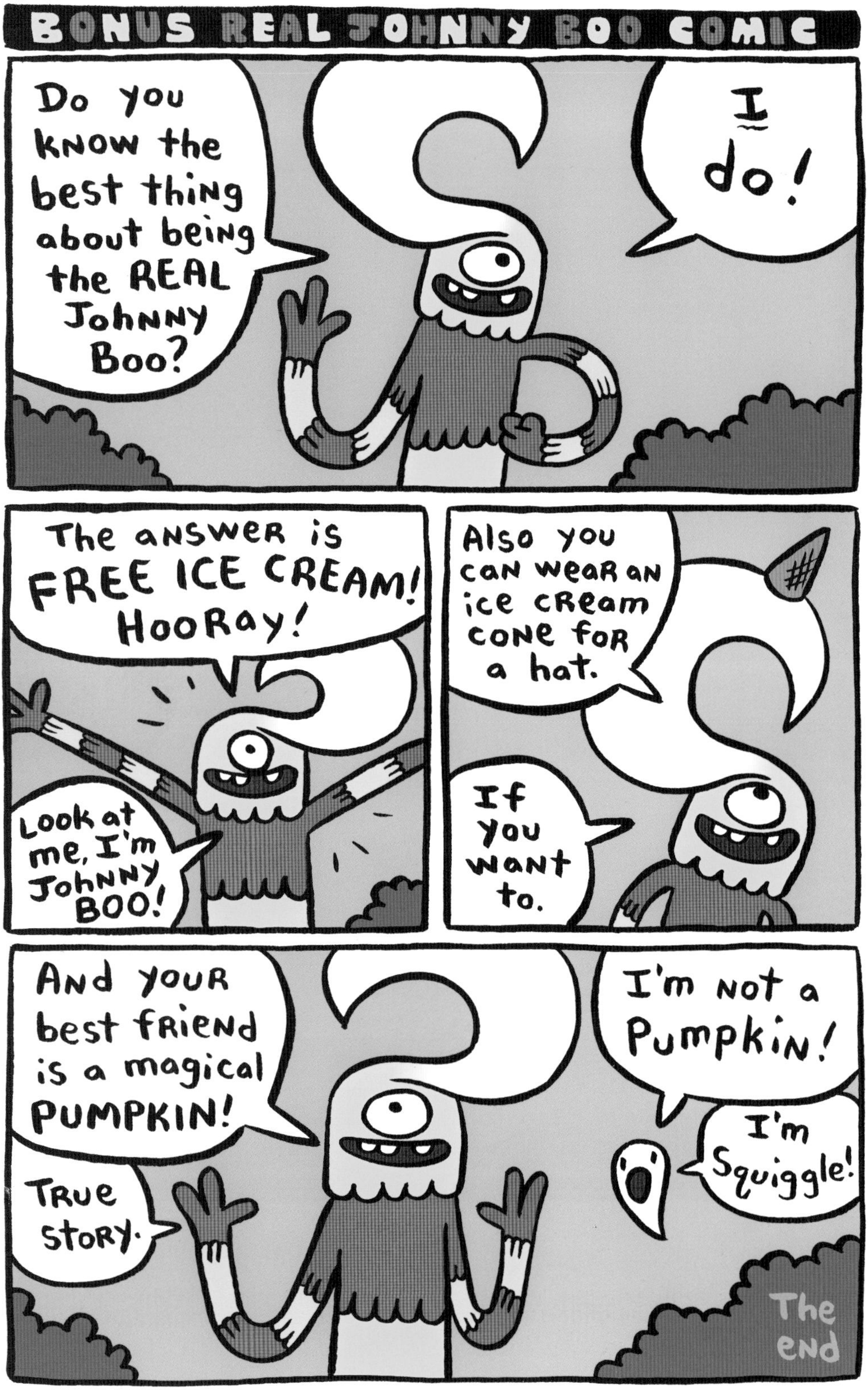
BONUS REAL JOHNNY BOO COMIC
Do you know the best thing about being the REAL Johnny Boo?
I do!
The answer is FREE ICE CREAM! HooRay!
Look at me, I'm Johnny BOO!
Also you can wear an ice cream cone for a hat.
If you want to.
And your best friend is a magical PUMPKIN!
True story.
I'm not a Pumpkin!
I'm Squiggle!
The end

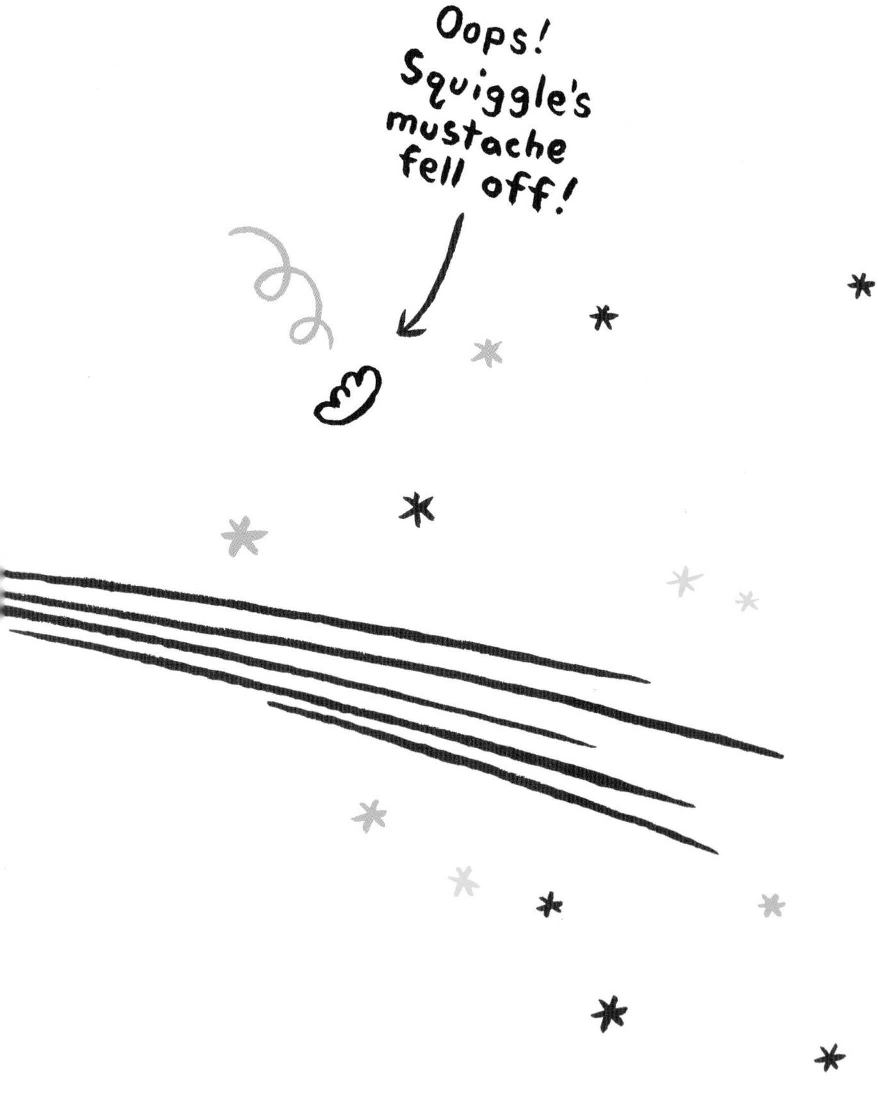
Oops! Squiggle's mustache fell off!

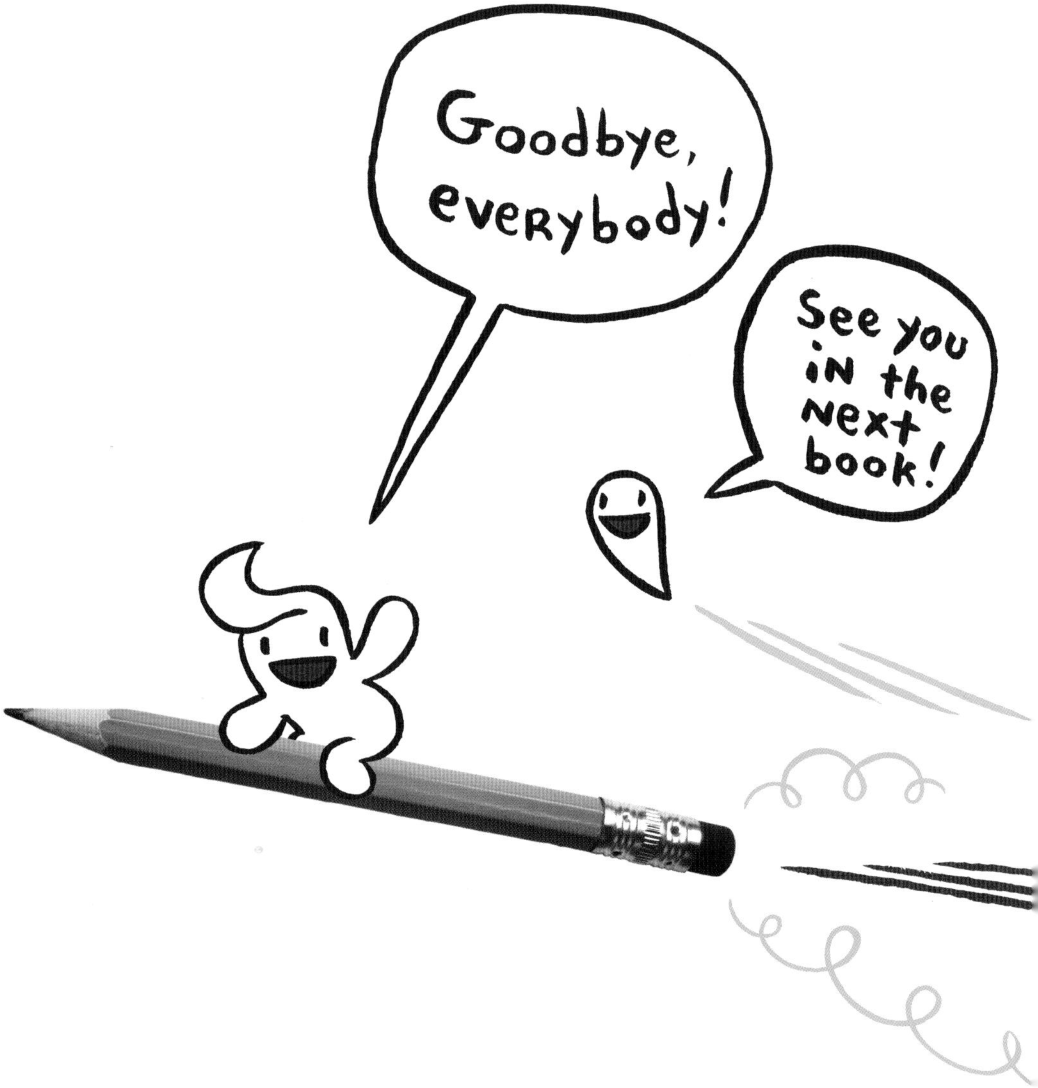
Goodbye, everybody!
See you in the next book!

THE AUTHOR

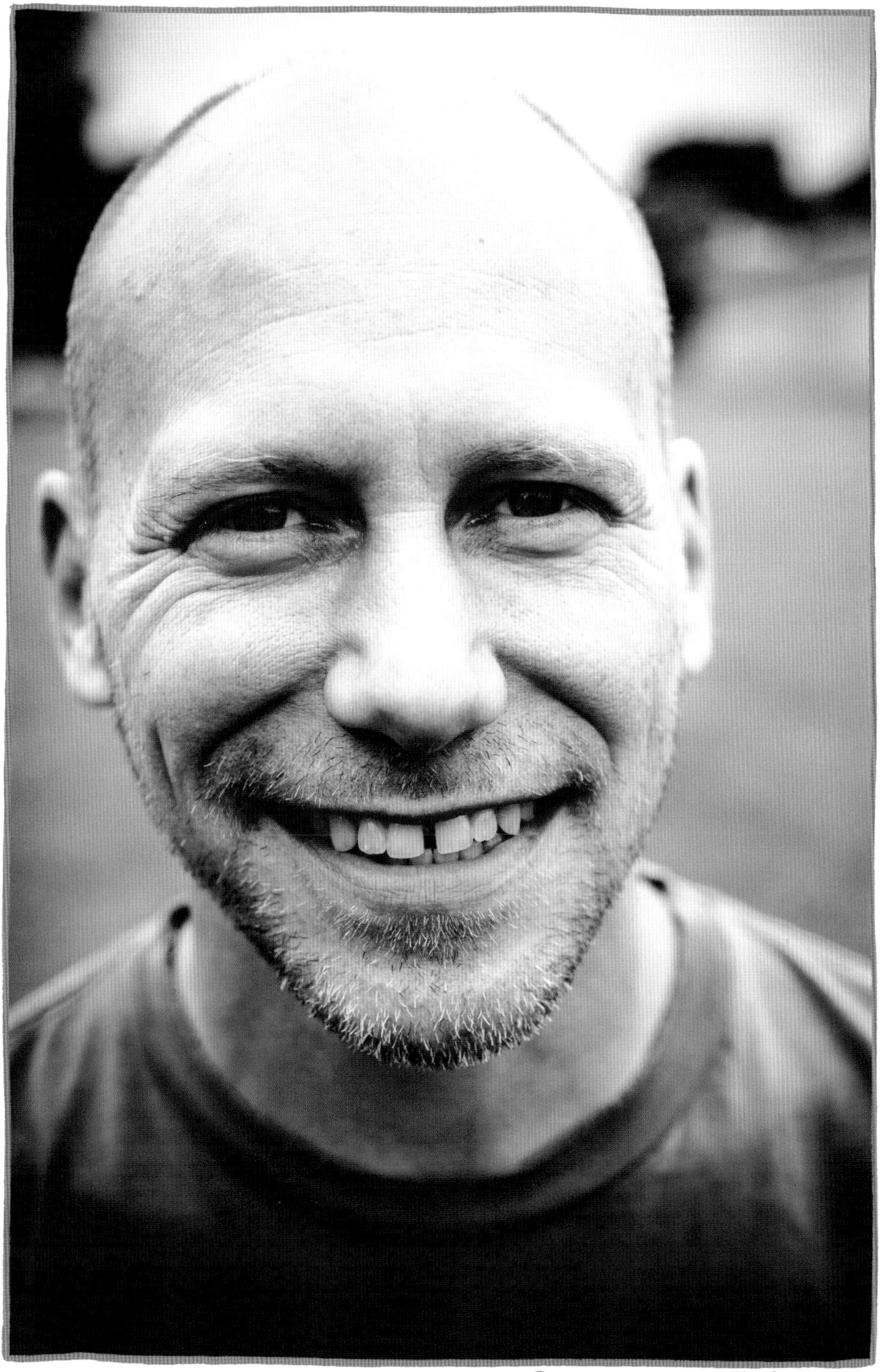

PHOTO BY SAM SIMON

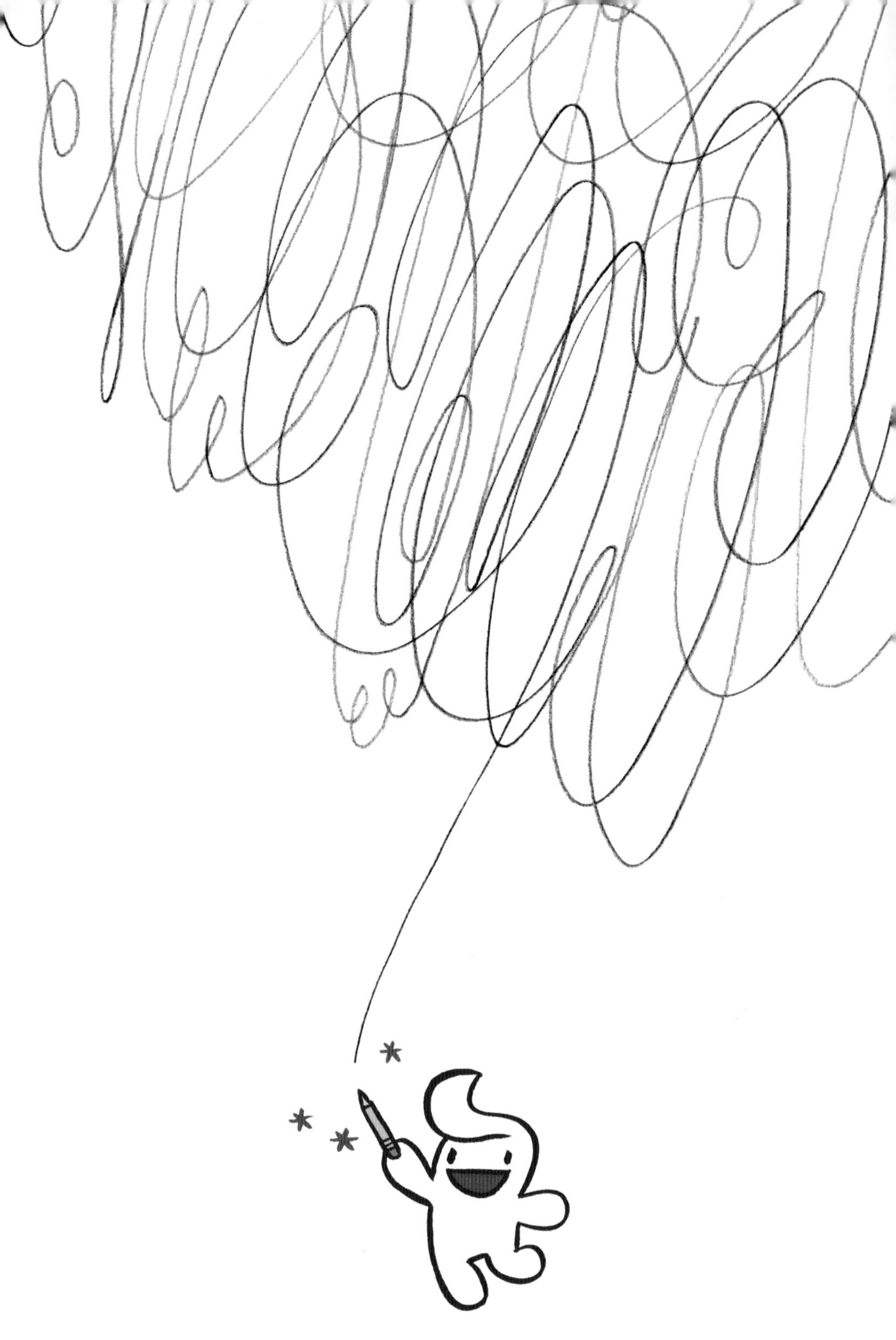